BECAUSE OF YOU

A CHRISTIAN ROMANCE

JULIETTE DUNCAN

WATER'S EDGE SERIES- BOOK 2

Cover Design by http://www.StunningBookCovers.com

Copyright © 2022 Juliette Duncan

All rights reserved.

NOTE FROM THE AUTHOR:

HELLO! Thank you for choosing to read this book - I hope you enjoy it! Please note that this story is set in Australia. Australian spelling and terminology have been used and are not typos!

As a thank you for reading this book, I'd like to offer you a FREE GIFT. That's right - my FREE novella, "Hank and Sarah - A Love Story" is available exclusively to my newsletter subscribers. Go to: http://www.julietteduncan.com/subscribe claim your copy now and to be notified of my future book releases. I hope you enjoy both books! Have a wonderful day!

Juliette

PROLOGUE

How could this have happened? How had she gotten it so wrong?

Jason had promised to love and cherish her, in sickness and in health, till death did they part.

Not just until his ex turned up and lured him away after one month of wedded bliss.

Tears were too good for him.

Numbness was her companion.

Her body, soul, and spirit were lifeless.

She read the Bible to gain comfort. If any were to be had.

But God had let her down.

She'd trusted Him. Or thought she had.

Hadn't He brought Jason into her life?

Or had she followed her heart when Jason Allsopp came to town and swept her off her feet?

The past seven months played in her mind until she wasn't sure what was real and what was made-up.

Had she only imagined she was in love?

She'd thought it was real. But what did she know? She'd never been in love before.

That day when she first laid eyes on him, her heart had flip-flopped like never before. His eyes were the colour of the sea, his hair, the colour of sand. Some said they could be twins.

He was new in town, and everybody loved him.

That's what they did in Water's Edge. Embraced new folk.

She fell for him after just one date. She'd been ready to fall in love. She knew it.

Her best friend had just married her brother, and she longed to have a love like theirs.

She'd acted recklessly.

Thrown rational thought aside.

Jumped in too quickly.

Convinced herself this was God's plan.

But it wasn't.

She didn't know Jason. Not really.

She thought she did.

He'd sat beside her in church. They'd attended Bible study together. They prayed together.

He said he didn't love Darlene anymore.

That it was over between them.

But it wasn't.

So why had he married *her*?

Willow breathed in. And out.

Everyone uttered condolences. Told her time was a great healer. God would bring someone better along.

But she caught their sideways glances. Their quiet whispers.

They blamed her for the failed marriage. If she'd been wife enough for him, he wouldn't have looked twice at Darlene.

She lived in Sydney, and although Willow had never met her, she'd heard things about the woman. Jason's move to Water's Edge was his fresh start.

He'd wanted to grow in the Lord.

Willow had never considered he might weaken and be drawn back to Darlene.

But he had.

Only one month after promising to love and cherish each other until death did they part, Willow watched her young marriage disintegrate.

She dropped her face into her hands, released a breath. Screamed into the darkness. "What did I do wrong, God? How did I end up in this situation? What's wrong with me?"

CHAPTER ONE

One year later

The bell over the front door of The Coffee Bean Café jangled. Willow Kelley looked up from behind the counter as Charlotte, owner of the local diner and a dear friend to just about everyone in Water's Edge, bustled inside.

With a cheery wave, Willow smiled at her friend. "Good morning, Charlotte. Your usual?"

"Of course. You know me so well." Charlotte chuckled as she reached the counter and settled onto a swivel stool.

Although anyone would have learned Charlotte's order after serving her every day for three years, Willow accepted the compliment. The older woman had been extra kind of late.

In a small town, everyone knew everyone else's business, so the fact that the past year hadn't been easy for Willow was no secret.

Being looked out for was nice. But the last thing she wanted was pity—although, if she'd been in the townspeople's shoes, *she* would've showered pity on herself.

Who wouldn't, after her husband of only one month walked out?

Could anything be more humiliating? Even now, her stomach churned every time she thought of it.

"How are things at the diner?" Willow angled her head as she pulled two espresso shots for Charlotte's flat white.

"Busy as usual." Charlotte toyed with the apple crumb pastry Willow had already placed on the counter. "It's been difficult to find a replacement for Amelia. She was such a reliable girl, and we sure miss having her around. But things change, and I'm delighted she can put time into her studies, work for Dr. Turner, *and* help Lucas at the Youth Centre. Working at the diner was just a stepping stone for that girl."

Though Willow was happy for her brother and sister-in-law, the reminder that some people got their happy ending pricked her heart as she frothed the milk for Charlotte's coffee. "She's enjoying her nursing studies."

Charlotte swivelled on her stool. "And how are *you* enjoying your schooling? You two girls are still carpooling to the city each week, aren't you?"

"We are." Willow rang up Charlotte's order at the register. "And it's going well."

Even to her ears, her tone sounded lackadaisical. For years, owning her own boutique had been her dream, and fashion design school was the first step in achieving that dream.

Classes had started right after she met Jason, and the course was everything she'd hoped it would be. But after he deserted her, she struggled to muster enthusiasm.

Charlotte's brow quirked. "If that's the case, why don't you sound more excited?"

It was foolish to try to pretend. This kind woman could see right through her. With her hair piled on her head creating a white halo and the softness around her wrinkled eyes, she looked like a grandmotherly guardian angel.

Willow shrugged. "You know why."

"I do." Charlotte's lips twisted, her features softening further. "Trials like the one you've endured do quite a number on just about every aspect of a person's life."

She had that right.

But although Willow understood the sentiment behind her words, she couldn't think of anyone else who'd gone through what she had. She didn't know *anyone* whose marriage had dissolved after one measly month.

She placed Charlotte's change on the counter. "It hasn't been easy, but life goes on."

"You're being very brave." Charlotte leaned in closer and patted her hand. "I know you have the support of your family, but if you ever need a shoulder to cry on, you know where to find me."

If only crying it out was all Willow needed.

Could the wounds from such a soul-destroying event ever heal?

Would she ever be able to move on? Learn to love again?

Would she ever be able to trust herself to make a good decision?

Would she ever be able to trust God again? Hear His voice? Know His will?

"Thanks, Charlotte." Willow rubbed the shivers from her bare arms, desperate to shift the conversation away from herself. "What do you have on the agenda for the day?"

"The first order of business is to get the guest bedroom ship-shape for my nephew. Declan's in between jobs and staying with me for a while. Did Lucas mention they've hired him to do some electrical work on the Youth Centre's new recreation room?"

"He did mention something about it," Willow replied half-heartedly. "It'll be nice for you to have company."

"Yes, it will." Charlotte sipped her espresso. "I'll introduce you as soon as possible. Although you might have already met."

A tiny flicker of interest lit inside her. "Oh?"

"He used to visit during the school holidays when he was just a lad."

"Hmm... maybe." Willow braced an elbow on the counter and, leaning over it, plopped her chin in her hand. She cared little about meeting new people. Or even ones she may have known. She wanted things to revert to the way they were before her heart was broken.

Back when she was happy.

Back when she trusted God.

By evening, Willow wanted to climb into bed, pull the covers over her head, and sleep until morning. Her divorce might be final, her marriage over, but the betrayal lingered.

But it was the Kelley family game night, and she had to go. Sure, she could explain to her parents she was still struggling and needed time alone. They'd understand. But she didn't want their pity, either.

She'd put on a brave face.

Soldier on.

Weep in secret.

After grabbing the potato salad she'd made the previous night, she shut the fridge, trudged out the door, climbed into her Toyota Prius, and headed for her parents' house. She barely noticed the pretty whitewashed homes with blue shutters and tubs of bright geraniums out front, nor the million-dollar ocean view from her parents' front porch.

As she stood there, a gust of wind caught her long blonde hair and whipped it across her face. Wedging the salad in the crook of her arm, she tucked the flyaway hair behind her ear while she kicked off her sandals.

She could still go home. It wasn't too late.

But Mum had heard her.

"Willow, is that you?"

"Yes, Mum." Steeling herself, Willow opened the screen door and followed the baked ham aroma to the kitchen.

Her mother looked up as Willow entered, her face pinching. "Darling, are you all right?"

Willow set the salad on the counter. "I'm fine."

"Hmm. I'm not so sure about that."

Her mother's soft tone sent Willow's emotions into a whirl once again. She sniffed. Turned her head.

Mum hurried around the counter, embraced her, and rubbed her back. "Hearts don't heal in a day or even a year, honey. Don't rush anything. Let yourself grieve."

Little choice about that with this constant cycle of grief and denial. She sniffed again. "I know."

"A family diversion is just what you need." Releasing her, Mum turned to the cupboard and grabbed a stack of plates. "It's Amelia's turn to supply the game tonight, so we're in for loads of fun. Dad's in the shower but will be down in a minute. Will you put these plates on the table, please?"

"Sure."

Amelia and Lucas arrived as Willow reached the dining room. She heard them before she saw them. As their happy sounds drifted her way, she released a heavy breath and set the table. She didn't begrudge them their happiness. It just magnified her loss—that's all.

"Hey, Willow." Amelia's smile was broad and warm as it always was these days. But a particular glow lit her this evening. Or was it that Willow felt so low?

"Hey, guys." Willow forced a smile. "Bring a game?"

"We sure did." Lucas's blue eyes sparkled. "Two, actually."

Great. She'd intended to slip out after one round of whatever game was selected. "Sounds fun."

Dad appeared in the doorway, his hair damp, his face clean-shaven and fresh. "Hey, kids. Everyone's here, huh?"

"Raring to go." Grinning, Amelia looked to Lucas, and they shared one of *those* smiles, the kind that only a couple deeply and madly in love could share.

Willow's shoulders drooped, and the heaviness in her chest pressed down further as she recalled the smile she and Jason had shared as they took their vows. He'd loved her then, hadn't he?

Dad poured a glass of iced tea from the pitcher on the side table. "How's school going, Amelia?"

She flicked a strand of brown hair over her shoulder. "Great, thanks. I'm loving every minute of it."

With pride in his eyes, Lucas slipped an arm around her waist. Kissed her cheek. "My wife's going to make the best nurse ever."

Willow couldn't agree more, but why did they need to be so lovey-dovey in front of her? She ground her teeth.

Mum arrived, carrying the ham. "I second that. You're going to be a wonderful nurse, Amelia."

"Thanks. I appreciate that. The ham looks delicious, Sheila."

"Let's get to it then, shall we?" Dad made a beeline for his seat.

If only Willow could summon an appetite and join wholeheartedly into the fun-loving companionship of her family, but she felt like an outsider looking in. She placed enough food on her plate to avoid comments from the others, especially her brother.

Once everyone had filled their plates and Dad had given thanks, Amelia presented her game selections. "Okay, tonight I've brought Candy Land and Hungry Hungry Hippos. Which do you want to start with?"

Curious glances flew around the table.

Mum pointed her fork at them. "No Scrabble?"

Amelia and Lucas shared a mischievous smile. "We thought we'd do something different tonight."

"Nothing wrong with going back to childhood." Dad speared a piece of ham with his fork. "With this ham so delicious, Shelia, I feel like a hungry hippo. I vote for that one."

"I second that," Mum piped up.

"What's your vote, Willow?" Amelia's gaze swung to her.

"Hungry Hippos sounds fun." Willow forced herself to reply, then averted her gaze.

"Good. That's what I was hoping you'd say." Amelia rubbed her hands together and then reached into the middle of the table and opened the game box. "Although Candy Land would be a useful game for Lucas to become familiar with, too. You have to be prepared for anything, don't you?"

What on earth? Willow eyed her sister-in-law, then met Mum's and Dad's confused gazes.

"Prepared? What do you mean?" Mum's brows lowered.

Amelia wiggled in her seat, looking ready to explode. "You

haven't guessed it yet? The child-themed games? Nothing?"

Pindrop silence followed before deafening excitement erupted.

"Amelia, you aren't!" Mum cried.

"I knew you two were up to something." Dad slapped his leg.

Willow responded using her inside voice. "Wait... Were the games your way of telling us you're pregnant?"

With her eyes alight, Amelia gave a nod.

Lucas's smile stretched from ear to ear as he slipped an arm around her shoulders. "Mum, Dad, you're going to be grandparents."

"And you're going to be an auntie, Willow," Amelia added, reaching for her hand. "You'll be the best auntie little Amelia or Lucas Jr. could ever hope for."

Willow sat back in her chair as the rest of the family stood to embrace each other. Joyous as the announcement was, emptiness dumped on her like a heavy rain cloud. When her parents stepped back, she had little choice but to stand and come forward. She managed a smile she hoped looked cheerful. "Congratulations, you two."

"How long have you known?" Mum asked as they all settled back down.

"Only a few days," Lucas answered. "We wanted nothing more than to tell you straightaway, but we also wanted to do it right and make it into a fun surprise."

"You certainly succeeded." Dad's deep chuckle rumbled like thunder from the rain cloud stalking Willow.

"It was a surprise to us as well." Amelia grasped Lucas's hand. "We weren't planning to start a family yet. With things so busy at the Youth Centre and me in school... I'm not sure how we're going to do it all."

"You'll find a way." Mum patted their clasped hands. "Young parents do it all the time. What a blessing. We're so happy for you both."

While her family chatted, Willow's throat tightened. When breathing became difficult, she excused herself and slipped down the hallway. Due to the thrill, the others seemingly thought little of it, for which she was grateful.

Closeting herself in the downstairs bathroom, she covered her mouth and quelled the sobs pressing against her chest.

Would this pain ever end?

As happy as she was for her brother and sister-in-law, their news highlighted her lost dreams, dreams she'd woven with Jason that would never come to fruition.

She scolded herself, even as fresh emotion clogged her throat. She swiped at the hot liquid streaming down her cheeks and grimaced at her red eyes in the mirror, even as her heart burned with the weight of her pain.

Get a grip. This is a big moment for Lucas and Amelia. Be happy for them.

Still, no matter how many times she told herself to stop making this about herself, the heaviness remained. She stayed in the bathroom until the grief threatening to overwhelm her subsided, leaving a dull ache. When she felt able to face her family again, she planted a smile on her face.

TWO

D eclan Ross had just finished changing the final light bulb in his aunt Charlotte's kitchen when she marched around the corner. Looking up at him, she wagged a finger. "I told you, changing the bulbs wasn't an emergency. You've only just arrived, Deckie. There's no reason to be slaving away already."

He stepped down from the ladder and gave her arm a fond pat. "I'm not slaving away. The bulbs needed changing, so I decided to do it while it was on my mind."

"I don't care. Chores can wait." She waved a hand towards the bedrooms. "Don't you have unpacking to do?"

"Yes, but I'd argue that, too, can wait."

Though she attempted to look strict, her mouth softened. "I'm so glad you agreed to come. It's been too long since you kept your old aunt company."

Yep. Way too long. He used to come to Water's Edge

during the holidays and stay with her for weeks on end. Mum would drive him down from the city, stay for a cup of tea with her older sister, and then head back, promising to collect him before school restarted.

He'd loved it here. Water's Edge was a great place for a boy to while away his holidays. He hung at the beach, rode his bike, and played cricket with the kids from church.

He never wanted to go home.

But that was years ago. Since then, he'd grown up, learned a trade, travelled. But then Dad left, and Mum needed him.

Yeah. Things hadn't been easy for her since Dad left her for his assistant. Declan got that. But she'd done nothing to dig herself out of the deep depression she'd sunk into.

He loved her, but after it going on so long, he needed a change of scenery before she pulled him down too. This job at Water's Edge had been a godsend he'd grabbed with both hands.

Perhaps he shouldn't have. Mum leaned on him for emotional support, but God knew he needed a break. She said she understood, even urged him to take the job, though he doubted she meant it. He promised to call and visit when he could. Water's Edge wasn't on the other side of the country, but rather an easy ninety-minute drive.

He returned his aunt's smile. "Thanks for having me."

She squeezed his arm. "The pleasure's all mine. But my goodness, I hadn't noticed how late it was. All the excitement of getting you settled in, I guess. I'll start dinner. I don't make it a habit to starve houseguests."

He chuckled. No one ever went hungry in her proximity. "Let me help."

She didn't protest this time. Her eyes glistened as she stepped towards him and slipped her arms around his waist. She was a tiny thing, and her white head rested against his chest. "It's nice having you here, Deckie."

He patted her back, inhaling her floral scent. "I'm glad, because you're stuck with me for the time being. I'm not needed at the Youth Centre until the day after tomorrow, so I'll have all of tomorrow to unpack. Now, let me help with dinner."

She eased away, looked up, and grinned. "Be my guest. Let's see if that sister of mine has taught you how to cook!"

IT TOOK ALL of ten minutes inside the Youth Centre for Declan to recognise Lucas and Amelia Kelley were fantastic people. Aunt Charlotte's praise for the couple behind the centre's success hadn't been exaggerated. Joy radiated from Lucas's face as he showed Declan around every room where he caught glimpses of the establishment's great work in action. Today, the young children, preschoolers, were enjoying the constructive and nurturing environment its founders created.

"Sure stays busy around here," he remarked as they completed their tour.

"Sure does." Lucas shared a smile with his wife. "That's why having this new rec room shipshape as soon as possible is so important. I can't thank you enough for putting us on your schedule. It means a lot."

"I should be thanking you. I'm grateful to have a project like this. It's come at the perfect time."

Amelia tucked a strand of hair behind her ear. "Charlotte's thrilled to have you in town. We had lunch at the diner the other day, and she was like a child preparing for Christmas morning as she told us about you coming."

Declan threw back his head and let out a peal of laughter. "She's a good aunt. And it's nice to be back."

Lucas clapped him on the shoulder. "Well, we're glad to have you. Would you like to inspect the rec room now?"

"Sure. Lead the way."

They headed to an area big enough for an indoor basketball court. The walls were unplastered—that would happen after he'd run the cables. "I won't know how much needs to be done until I've had a chance to do a thorough inspection, but I estimate we'll have it up and running by month's end."

With its high roof, the room echoed when he talked.

"That's great." Amelia smiled. "It can't come soon enough. We seem to be outgrowing our existing space more and more every day."

"Aunt Charlotte told me how much you two do for the kids. Sounds like you give them a home away from home. You have a heart for the young."

Lucas slipped an arm around Amelia's shoulders, his eyes glinting. "We ought to. We're soon to have one of our own."

Declan's brows lifted. He looked between the pair. "You're

expecting? Congratulations!"

"Thank you." Amelia beamed as she leaned into Lucas. "We can hardly believe it, but yes, we're thrilled."

Declan shoved his hands into his pockets. A baby, huh? They were his age and about to become parents. He was behind the hot wire on that one since he didn't even have a girlfriend. Not that he was in a hurry.

He scanned the unfinished rec room once more. "This is going to be a great area for the kids. The town needs a place like this where they can hang out safely and not get caught up in drugs and stuff."

"That's our aim, isn't it, Amelia?" Lucas smiled and rubbed her arm.

She nodded. "Yes. We've been blessed with funding. Otherwise, it would still be a pipe dream."

"Well, I'm raring to get started."

They shook hands. Declan congratulated the couple again before Lucas and Amelia headed to other parts of the centre, leaving him to stroll to his truck, grab his tools, and make a start.

Willow had always enjoyed carpooling with Amelia. Having undivided time to catch up with her sister-in-law was a high-light of her week, a time when they shared their dreams and enjoyed each other's company.

After Jason left, Amelia was the one person Willow could

be honest with. The one who knew how deep her hurt ran. She put on a brave face with everyone else, even Mum and Dad, but with Amelia, Willow could be herself.

But today, all Amelia wanted to talk about was the baby. Didn't she understand what it was doing to her?

Willow listened to her chatter, giving a nod here, a smile there.

Just when she thought her smiling and nodding put up a sufficient cover for her sadness, Amelia stopped and faced her. "I'm sorry, Willow. I've been talking nonstop."

No joke. Willow forced another smile. Held her hands rigid on the steering wheel. "It's fine. You're excited. I want to hear all about it, really."

Amelia's face crumpled. "I don't doubt that. But it was insensitive of me."

A knot formed in Willow's stomach the way it did whenever anyone showed her pity. Even Amelia. "Just because my husband ran off with another woman doesn't mean we can't talk about the things that are going well for you."

Amelia reached out and squeezed her wrist. "Maybe. But I know how much you're still struggling, and me expecting a baby will only make it worse."

Willow released a dry chuckle. Focusing on the road ahead, she forced down the anger, bitterness, and self-recrimination circling in her head like vultures. "Don't worry about it. The memories are always lurking, ready to jump out and pummel me."

"I'm so sorry, Willow."

"Yeah, me too." Was that even her voice? Before Jason left, she'd never sounded so toneless. "But it is what it is."

Amelia turned down the radio. "You've been very brave. But you don't always have to be so strong, you know."

Willow exhaled. "If I'm not, I won't be able to go on. Besides, having the baby to plan for will get my mind off myself." The knot in her empty stomach tightened, heavy and hard until she wanted to curl over it protectively. She might never have children, but the baby Amelia was carrying was flesh and blood. But would being an auntie assuage her deepest longings of having her own child? "I can't wait to be an auntie."

The pop song whined about an unfaithful love. Amelia winced and switched to a worship station, keeping the volume low. "There's so much to do. We weren't expecting to start a family yet, so although it's exciting and we feel very blessed, it's also overwhelming."

Willow waved a dismissive hand in her sister-in-law's direction. "If you're worried you won't be able to juggle it all, I have no doubt you will. You and Lucas already do a million things at once. How different can adding a baby to the equation be?"

Amelia burst into laughter, her eyes sparkling. "Yeah, how hard can it be? Piece of cake, right?"

"Right."

Just when Willow thought they'd left the topic of her pain, Amelia returned to it.

"I want to say one more thing about the past, Willow. Just

because your happy ending didn't turn out the way you expected, it doesn't mean wonderful things aren't in store for you. God hasn't forgotten to fulfill His purpose for your life. He's not going to leave you wallowing in the wilderness forever. He's going to lead you into an amazing future. You have to trust Him."

And therein lay the problem. *Could* she trust God again?

More than anything, she wanted to believe that she had a future and a hope, that God wouldn't leave her in this valley forever, that He had a beautiful plan for her life. But how could she if she didn't trust Him?

Jason had been His beautiful plan, or so she'd thought.

But had she been so focused on marrying him she hadn't stopped and listened? Truly sought God's guidance? If she had, might He have whispered that Jason wasn't the one He'd intended for her?

Was it her fault she was in this miry pit?

Not to distress Amelia with her gloomy thoughts, she sent her sister-in-law a smile. "Thanks for your encouragement. It's always appreciated."

She drove on towards the city. Engaged in small talk. Dropped Amelia at the nursing wing of the University campus. Parked under a shady tree outside the Fashion Design School. Worked hard to summon the determination to march inside and do what she'd come to do.

Help me to trust You again, Lord. Help me let go of the bitterness and anger weighing me down. And help me to forgive Jason. And myself.

CHAPTER

THREE

Sunday mornings had always been Willow's favourite day of the week. She loved going to church, worshipping her Lord in song, having her soul fed by the message, fellowshipping with other believers.

She'd loved it even more when Jason started coming with her. During their courtship and month-long marriage, she'd grown accustomed to having the person she believed to be her life partner by her side, worshipping God with her.

But today, as she sat in the car park willing herself to go in, the burden of walking in alone felt almost too heavy to stand up against. Without permission, her mind wandered back to one such Sunday morning....

The freshness of the spring air floated into the sanctuary as the members of the Water's Edge community filed into the church to mingle before the service. Willow's heart soared with the fellowship of her close friends. Deep in conversation about an upcoming wedding, she didn't notice Jason until he stood right beside her.

"There you are," he whispered in her ear. "I was looking for you."

Her heart fluttering, she turned to him with a ready smile. "Were you?"

"Always." He kissed the tip of her nose.

Heat flooded her cheeks at the love in his eyes. "Did you find a place to sit?"

"I did. You coming?"

"Always." She took his hand, said goodbye to her friends, and followed him through the crowded room. They reached their place in a middle pew while the worship team stepped onto the stage.

Music soaked into her soul. Being in this place with fellow worshippers and the man she loved brought her such joy. Holding his hand, feeling its strength encompass hers, she couldn't help but wonder what it would be like to enter this sacred place for another reason—their wedding. She'd always dreamed of walking down the aisle with her church family surrounding her. She looked at Jason's handsome profile, love filling her. The thought of this man waiting for her at the altar was more incredible than anything she could imagine. One day soon. One day soon...

PULLING HERSELF FROM HER REVERIE, Willow smoothed her hands along the black-and-white striped skirt she'd paired with a ruffled white blouse and red accessories to match her lipstick. She'd taken special care in selecting her outfit today. Not because she had to impress—her outward appearance wouldn't make her any more acceptable in the eyes of the Lord. She'd chosen her outfit because months had passed since she'd found joy in piecing together the perfect outfit. Before Jason, fashion had been her everything. After his betrayal, she'd cared little about what she wore.

She'd hoped assembling an outfit would boost her spirits, yet dread over entering the church building lingered. Although the people of Water's Edge didn't judge her, she couldn't help feeling conspicuous amidst the congregation.

Her eyes slid shut. "Lord, please give me the strength to go inside. Let the comfort I used to receive from being in Your house return. I need to know You have a plan in all of this."

Entering late would be more conspicuous. She inhaled deeply, gathered her purse and Bible, and opened the car door.

Lifting her chin, she strode towards the entrance. After months of wearing flats, her high heels felt awkward. Uncomfortable, even. Had it been that long?

She slipped into a back-row seat as the first worship song began. Then Lucas's strong tenor and smooth guitar cued the rest of the worship team, and her heart calmed. From behind the microphone, Amelia added her sweet soprano voice to the melody of the old hymn as the congregation stood to join in.

I hear the Saviour say,
"Thy strength indeed is small

25

Child of weakness, watch and pray
Find in Me thine all in all"
Jesus paid it all
All to Him I owe;
Sin had left a crimson stain,
He washed it white as snow.

Sin had left its crimson stain.... It sure had. Everyone told her Jason sinned when he left her for another woman. She couldn't disagree. But that stain had seeped into her heart and was still lingering there.

Could the stain be washed? Could she rediscover her all in all in Jesus? Her strength indeed was small.

Lord, help me find myself in You again.

The following praise songs washed over her soul, giving her hope. Pastor Noah's sermon provided further assurance.

"'Know therefore that the Lord your God is God; He is the faithful God, keeping His covenant of love to a thousand generations of those who love Him and keep His commandments.'

"Regardless of how devastating your situation might seem, be assured that God is working to shape for you a victorious and fulfilling future. As the prophet Jeremiah tells us, God's plans for us are good and include a hopeful and purpose-filled future. Start expecting. Somewhere in the rubble of your situation, you'll find 'a staff' shaped for you by God, just as Moses did.

"Trusting is believing in the promises of God in all circumstances, especially in those where the evidence seems to be to the contrary. God's goodness isn't based on our present situation. The seasons of life include both good and bad times. Life is filled with contrasts. We go through mountains, and we go through valleys. We go through successes, and we go through failures. We have wins, and we have losses. But nothing —*absolutely nothing*—can change the fact that God is good, He loves you, and He will never leave you. Will you pray with me?"

Willow bowed her head. Closed her eyes. Inhaled slowly.

"Lord God, creator of heaven and earth, we come humbly before You, acknowledging Your sovereignty. So often, we struggle to see Your hand at work in our lives, and yet it's in those times when we feel lost, unloved, and unsure of what lies ahead, that You carry us. You always have our back, Lord. Help us to remember that. Help us to look up. To trust You, to keep our eyes on You. Give us greater trust, deeper faith, and expectant hearts as we wait for You to fulfill Your promises in our lives. In Jesus' precious name, we pray. Amen."

"Amen." Willow brushed her eyes. Opened them. How did God know what she needed to hear? Perhaps He did have her back.

Mum arrived, slipped onto the seat beside her, and kissed her cheek. "Dad and I saved you a seat up front."

Willow grimaced. "Sorry, I was running late."

"You look nice."

"Thank you. The sermon was good."

Mum nodded. "I think it was meant for you."

"You might be right."

Mum's gaze swept the sanctuary. "Amelia and Lucas are around somewhere. There've been so many people asking about the baby, I've had a hard time keeping track of who they're talking to. Oh, there they are. Is that Charlotte's nephew Declan they're with?"

Willow located the man. Medium height, short dark hair, day-old beard. Genuine smile. But was it genuine? How would she know? She didn't trust herself to make good judgements anymore.

"Charlotte said Lucas and Amelia feel fortunate he was available to work on the rec room. He sounds like an extremely sharp man," Mum went on.

"Good timing, then."

Lizzy, a young woman from Bible study, jumped into the conversation with Declan, her face eager. He had charisma. That was for sure. He wouldn't want for female attention.

But after what Willow had been through, Lizzy's open flirting seemed so frivolous.

Would Willow ever return to that level of blissful naivety? With how a love she'd believed to be pure and lasting had soured, she doubted she'd ever indulge in the simple enjoyment of butterflies and easygoing banter again.

Mum stood and looped her arm through hers. "Why don't we go over and introduce ourselves? We want to make sure he feels welcome."

Great. Willow barely felt social enough to converse with

the people she already knew, let alone someone she didn't. "Mum…"

"Come on. It'll do you good."

Mum all but dragged her to the gathering. Lizzy had just broken off and was speaking with someone else. A small mercy. Not that Willow wanted to vie for Declan's attention.

"Sheila, Willow!" Amelia stepped towards them. "Great to see you. Have you met Declan yet?"

Mum shook her head. "We haven't, but we plan to remedy that straightaway." She held out her hand to the newcomer. "Hello, Declan. I'm Sheila, Lucas's mother. We've heard so much about you."

"Really?" Declan chuckled as he shook her hand.

"All good things—don't you worry. If you haven't figured it out yet, your aunt thinks the world of you."

A sparkle lit his brown eyes, and perfect white teeth flashed against tanned skin with his open, friendly smile. "I'm not sure why."

"Don't be so modest. From all reports, we're lucky to have you here. Welcome." Mum tugged Willow forward. "This is my daughter, Willow."

His brow lifted. "Willow? It's nice to meet you."

Those eyes. Ugh! How had just one look from him made her twitterpated?

"And you." She forced a smile and nearly groaned as heat crept up her neck.

His mouth quirked.

Get a grip. Any single woman in Water's Edge would buckle at the knees if he looked at them like that.

She brushed her foolishness aside.

"Willow works at The Coffee Bean Café here in town," Mum chimed in. "So, if you're ever in the mood for a stupendously good latte, you know where to go."

"Noted." He flashed another brilliant smile.

Amelia and Lucas went on to talk about the rec room plans and how quickly Declan had taken to the work. Willow slipped away from the group.

Charlotte's nephew seemed a kind man, handsome, too. He did look familiar, but maybe she just imagined it.

Any other time, she might've been eager to know him, but once bitten, twice shy. Besides, God still had work to do on her heart, which was too heavy to contemplate any romantic notions right now.

Mum had been correct about church being the place to bring her heavy heart, but she was ready to go home, ponder the sermon, and perhaps make peace with God. After slipping out the side door, she reached her car before anyone had a chance to stop her.

FOUR

By the end of the first full week working at the Youth Centre, Declan was ahead of schedule, making him optimistic. Having a project all his own to focus on, rather than working to a boss's agenda, felt good.

He'd used his busyness during this settling-in period as an excuse not to call Mum. She'd been on his mind, but once he spoke with her, she'd put the guilts on him, even though she'd encouraged him to take the job. He couldn't win.

Now, sitting on Aunt Charlotte's front porch with a glass of iced tea, he couldn't put the call off any longer. He pulled out his phone and found Mum's number. She picked up on the third ring.

"Hi, Mum. It's me."

"Well, well, I was wondering when you'd call."

He bristled. Closed his eyes. Why did she always criticise him? Hurt people tended to bleed on the people who hadn't cut them, and Mum's wounds were still raw, even after two years.

"Sorry. Things have been busy here." He drew a line in the condensation of the rosebud spray design on his iced tea glass. "But I'm settling in well and have started work at the Youth Centre."

No response. Not that he'd expected one.

He cleared his throat. "How are you doing?"

"It's quiet around here, but I'm used to it."

There it was again. The barb.

"Will it work if I visit next weekend? I should be able to get away."

"Only if you want to. I don't want to be any trouble."

Yeah. Sure. "It's no trouble. When I took this job, I told you I'd make a point of visiting."

"No need to feel obliged. Work keeps me busy."

Declan pinched the bridge of his nose with two fingers. Keeping busy during weekdays was something, but it wouldn't relieve the ache she battled when she came home to an empty house. There was no escaping that. As he always did these days when speaking with her, he prayed for wisdom to help alleviate that pain. To make sure she knew he cared. "I *want* to visit, Mum. I *want* to make sure you're all right."

"Of course, I'm all right."

Lord, give me patience.

At their usual impasse, he clinked the ice in his glass, letting the soft sound soothe him. He did his best to be there for her but not get too close while she denied she needed his support even as she silently screamed just how much she needed it. Crazy.

"That doesn't change my mind about wanting to visit. I'll keep you posted about when I'll arrive so you can clear your schedule."

Her bitter laugh jarred him, and tea sloshed up the sides of his glass.

"As if I have a social calendar to clear. You know I don't, Declan."

He sat back. Before him, the setting sun cast brilliant orange and red streaks across the sky. From a nearby tree, cockatoos screeched, drowning out the ocean's whoosh. He rubbed between his eyes again. Time to step onto precarious ground since they were getting nowhere tiptoeing around it. "You need to get out, Mum. Make some new friends if you don't want to see your old ones. It's important. You'll feel better."

"I suppose all I need is a few close friends to guide me right out of the haze of betrayal your father left, right? Do you think that would make everything better?"

"No." He pressed the cool glass to the throbbing at his temple. "But you wouldn't feel so alone. Being left alone with bitter thoughts is a dangerous thing. Things can spiral downwards quickly."

"Spiral downwards? If you haven't noticed, things can't get much lower."

A heavy breath escaped him. He moved the glass to his other temple. "What about visiting Vera? I saw on Facebook that her daughter got married recently."

"I was invited to the wedding."

"But you didn't go."

"I didn't feel like it."

"You might have enjoyed it if you'd gone."

"Doubt it. I don't need to connect with people. Lonely or not, keeping to myself is the best option, thank you very much."

Ouch.

She'd always been a determined woman. Now she'd turned that determination into a desire to stay buried in her depression—as if by keeping the hurt alive she could get back at Dad. At least she still went to work, although she took plenty of sick days. So many, he was surprised she still had the job. And she'd pushed God away. He let out the breath he'd been holding. He could do little other than be there for her and pray for her, trusting that one day she'd turn a corner.

He wouldn't lose hope.

"Okay. I'll check with you again before coming next weekend. Goodnight, Mum."

He remained on the porch after ending the call. He'd known it would be like this.

But attending church today had confirmed his peace in coming to Water's Edge. The message had spoken to him, and the peoples' kindness spurred his passion for the Lord. This was where he was supposed to be, for now at least, surrounded by godly folk like Aunt Charlotte, Lucas, and Amelia.

His thoughts wandered to Willow, Lucas's sister. He might remember her from when he was a kid, but he had no eyes for girls then, even ones who looked like her.

She'd had a reticence about her when they were introduced. Her smile held sadness. Her long blonde hair, paired with her classy outfit, had caught his attention. He didn't know much about women's fashion, but she had a flair for it. He'd planned to strike up a deeper conversation with her, but she'd slipped out. Another time, maybe.

Aunt Charlotte stepped onto the porch bearing a pitcher of iced tea. "I thought you might need a refill."

"Thanks." He offered a grateful smile as he held out his glass.

She filled it before settling on the bench beside him. "Did you get a hold of your mum?"

He nodded.

"How... how is she?"

How did one even answer that? He twisted the glass in his grip. "She's all right. The same, I'd say."

His aunt placed a comforting hand on his arm and gave a light squeeze. "Don't give up hope, Declan. Sometimes, giving people the time they need to heal is all we can do, even when we want nothing more than to make everything better in a single moment."

"Yes." He released a heavy breath. Ran his hand across his hair. "And inner healing's God's work, isn't it? Not ours."

Aunt Charlotte patted his arm. "Exactly. We're called to love and support, but we can't make things happen. That's up to God, but so often, we place the burden on ourselves, to our detriment."

Yep. Hadn't he been doing that for the past two years?

A companionable silence fell as the sky darkened.

Aunt Charlotte was right. He needed to do just that, difficult as it was. As much as he loved his mother, he had a life to live. Dreams to follow. He couldn't follow them if he spent every non-working hour with her.

Lord, bless my mum. Help her to look to You for comfort. Lift her from the miry pit she's found herself in. Let her learn to forgive and let go of the bitterness burying her. Help her find peace and purpose by turning to You.

CHAPTER
FIVE

"Knock, knock." Willow pushed open the door to Dr. Turner's medical clinic with her elbow and tried not to spill the three coffees in the cardboard tray.

"Who's there?" Amelia answered from the back.

"Willow."

"Willow, who?"

By the time she located Amelia in the storeroom, Willow was chuckling, and it felt good. "Willow, your sister-in-law. Remember, your ex-roommate? Ringing a bell yet?"

Amelia waved a hand. "Of course, it does. Sorry I've been MIA lately. It was weird not carpooling to Sydney this week."

"It's okay. I understand." Willow handed her a coffee and dropped into one of the plastic chairs opposite the exam table. "You've been busy, and with the change in your prac schedule, going together didn't work. We'll get back to it soon. How are things with the baby?"

Amelia pulled a packet of gauze from the box she was unpacking. "My mood's changing all the time. Joy, panic, anxiety, and back to joy faster than I ever thought possible."

Willow flicked her hair back and freed Amelia's coffee from the tray. "I guess that's to be expected. You'd know that as well as anyone since you're practically a nurse."

Amelia folded both hands around the paper cup and brought it to her nose, inhaling deeply but not taking a sip yet. "And Dr. Turner's assured me it's all quite normal."

"Speaking of Dr. Turner, where is he? Are you holding down the fort?"

"Just for another half hour or so. He's doing a couple of house calls but will be back for this afternoon's appointments. Thanks so much for bringing the coffee. I'll heat his when he comes in."

"You're welcome." Willow was about to ask Amelia if she was free for lunch and a catch-up when the front door opened.

"Doc?" Amelia called.

"No, it's me. Charlotte."

"Doc's not here," Amelia answered as, coffees in hand, she and Willow made their way out of the storeroom to the front. "It's just us for now."

Charlotte held the arm of a young woman Willow didn't recognise. She looked barely out of high school. Perspiration dotted the line of the dishevelled black hair she'd tied into a ponytail at the top of her thin neck. Although she wore a baggy sweatshirt, her baby bump protruded.

After thrusting her coffee at Willow, Amelia hurried

forward and supported the girl's other side. "Hi, I'm Amelia. What seems to be the trouble?"

"I found this young lady outside the diner," Charlotte spoke as they guided her to a seat. "I think she's having false labour pains."

"I'm sure it's nothing," the young woman mumbled.

"Let's get you checked, anyway," Amelia replied. "Charlotte knows her stuff, and I don't want to take any chances. Let's see what's going on, okay?"

When the young woman nodded, Amelia helped her back to her feet. "Willow, will you get the door?"

Hurrying around the trio, Willow elbowed the door open. Charlotte and Amelia helped the young woman onto the examination table.

"What's your name, sweetie?" Amelia picked up a blank paper chart and a pen. "I don't think we've met."

"Courtney." Her voice came out small. "I've just moved in with my grandad."

"Oh, who's he?" Charlotte's brows lifted.

"Ricky. Ricky Smith."

The three other women exchanged glances. A peevish old man, Ricky Smith mostly kept to himself.

"And how are you liking it? Staying with your grandad, I mean." Lips pressing tight, Amelia filled in that information.

Courtney shrugged. Her eyes moistened. "It's okay, I guess."

"It doesn't look like it's all right." Charlotte produced a

travel-sized packet of tissues from her purse and handed them to the girl.

After wiping her eyes and blowing her nose, Courtney drew a shaky breath. "He was furious when he discovered I was pregnant. He says I'm a disgrace to the family."

Amelia's lips pressed tighter. "And what do your parents have to say?"

The girl ducked her head, her shoulders hunching up by her neck. "My parents died in a car crash years ago. I was living with my great aunt until she passed away. I have no one besides my grandad."

Amelia touched her arm. "I'm sorry you're not receiving more support, but Dr. Turner and I will do everything to ensure you and your little one get the best of care. Have you met the doctor yet?"

Courtney shook her head, her face pale, her jaw twitching.

"No need to be frightened—the doctor's kind and understanding. He'll be here soon." Smiling warmly, Amelia rubbed the girl's back. "Since you've carried on a conversation with us for this long, I'm guessing you're not in labour. I'll give you an initial examination, and Dr. Turner will take it from there when he arrives."

With a nudge, Charlotte guided Willow towards the door. "Come on. We'll wait out front."

Willow set aside Amelia's coffee, then gripped her cooling one with both hands, twisting it in her grip as they waited on the plastic waiting room chairs. "She looked so scared."

"My heart aches for her."

They stood when Dr. Turner entered, gave them a nod, and removed his hat. "Well, this is a nice surprise, but where's Amelia?"

"In the back with a patient, a young woman named Courtney," Charlotte supplied. "She's been waiting for you."

"Oh?" He tipped his head to one side. "Your expressions tell me it's serious. I'd better go see."

A few moments later, Amelia joined them.

"How is she?" Willow stood again, eager to hear how the poor girl was doing.

A breath slid loose from Amelia. "Both she and the baby seem okay, thankfully, but she's in a difficult place. I know what it's like to be without a support system. I ache for her."

Amelia had become so much a part of Water's Edge that Willow sometimes forgot she'd been a newcomer not so long ago. It seemed she'd always been here, but when Charlotte found her outside the bar three years ago, Amelia had been lost, lonely, and lacking a support system of any kind. No wonder she empathised.

"There's no way she'll be able to stay with Ricky once the baby's born," Amelia continued. "If he's angry about the pregnancy, it's unlikely he'll support them."

Charlotte stepped forward and gripped Amelia's upper arms. "I'll make sure she's taken care of. The town folk will pull together."

"Thank you, Charlotte. You're such a kind woman." Although Amelia smiled, sadness dimmed her brown eyes. "What a rocky situation that innocent child is being brought into. Thinking of all the struggles he or she will face hurts my heart. It won't be an easy road, no matter how much support Courtney's offered."

"At least we're all here to help." Willow had to pause when her voice caught in her throat. "You have such a heart for others, Amelia. You truly feel their pain."

Amelia's smile wobbled. "It's just... I was her once. I might not have been pregnant, but I was very much alone. And I haven't forgotten how that felt."

Willow's chest swelled. "You and Lucas are going to make such great parents."

"I second that." Charlotte nodded. "He or she is blessed indeed."

Amelia brushed her eyes. "Thank you."

Charlotte glanced at her watch. "I'd like to stay until Dr. Turner finishes his exam, but I have to get back to the diner."

"I'll see she gets home safely." Willow sipped her luke-warm coffee. Yuck. She'd have to reheat it, but for now, at least it still smelled good.

"Thanks. I'll check with her in a day or so. See you later, girls." Charlotte gave a backwards wave, but then paused, and turned. "We should do a baby basket for her."

"Great idea." Amelia's face brightened. "And I've just decided... I'll be her support person during her labour."

Whoa. Willow nearly jostled her coffee cup. "Are you sure about that?"

"Absolutely. She has no one else. It's the least I can do."

"Goodness, Amelia. You're going above and beyond."

"Isn't that what you two did for me?"

Willow's forehead creased. "Maybe, but we didn't go through childbirth with you."

"But you *did* go through another kind of birth with me, for which I'm forever grateful. The Lord's leading me to do this. Besides, I want to."

Charlotte stepped forward and hugged her. "God bless you, Amelia. The Lord led me to that girl, just like He led me to you. His ways are beyond measure."

"They certainly are."

Alone with her sister-in-law, Willow gave up on her coffee and faced Amelia. "Are you sure? It's a huge thing."

"I'm almost a nurse, and I've done a midwifery rotation. It's a no-brainer."

"I guess you're right. You'll do great. I'll help with the basket—I can do that."

Dr. Turner and Courtney exited the consultation room. The girl's hazel eyes were still dull.

"Is everything all right?" Willow looked to Courtney and then to the doctor.

"Everything's fine. The baby's due in eight weeks, and he or she has a healthy heartbeat." He patted Courtney on the back. "I'm sending her for an ultrasound and some blood tests. I guess you girls wouldn't care to take her?"

Willow looked to Amelia. Shrugged. "I have nothing else on."

"Neither do I."

"It's settled then," Willow said. "We can take my car."

"Thanks, girls. I knew you'd look after her." He turned to Courtney. "I'll see you in two days' time unless you're concerned about anything." He patted her back again. "And don't worry, you'll be fine."

With a nod and a soft thank you, she followed Willow and Amelia outside. Courtney said little as they drove to the hospital. Dr. Turner had called ahead and booked her in for her ultrasound. Willow waited outside the room while Amelia accompanied her. It made sense. Not only was Amelia almost a nurse, but she was also expecting a child. She had a lot more in common with the girl than Willow did.

Once again, a leaden weight crashed on Willow. Courtney might not have the support of the baby's father or her grandfather, but she carried new life inside her. How amazing would that be? Soon, she'd have a tiny baby to love and cherish. Despite her having little else, the town folk would ensure both she and the baby were cared for and loved. She had something to live for.

Sometimes, like right now, Willow wondered what *she* had to live for.

Lord, You promised me a future and a hope. Please give me strength so I can carry on and not feel left behind, because right now, that's how I feel.

CHAPTER
SIX

Declan stepped back from the electrical box in Aunt Charlotte's diner and closed it with a satisfying click. Electrical odds and ends she hadn't been aware of had needed attention. Of course, she'd told him they could wait and his work at the Youth Centre took priority, but he'd gotten her nod to move forward on his day off.

With the lunch rush over, only a few customers remained in the dining room. Waitresses brewed fresh pots of coffee and checked on the customers while Aunt Charlotte busied herself placing sweet goodies onto a foiled-lined tray.

Dropping onto a stool, he rested his arms on the polished reclaimed-timber counter. "You're all up to code on your electrical now. The place isn't going to burn down any time soon."

"Wonderful!" She lifted her gaze and beamed. "What can I get you for your trouble? A hamburger? Milkshake? Sundae?"

"A cup of that freshly brewed coffee with cream would be perfect." He scanned the rows of red and pink fondant hearts on the tray. "What's all this?"

"Adornments for the pastries we'll be selling at the Easter Extravaganza." She set a steaming mug on the counter in front of him.

He took a long sip of the fragrant drink. "Easter Extravaganza, huh? Sounds big."

"It sure is." Smiling, she returned to the hearts. "The church hosts it, but all of Water's Edge gets involved. It brings the community together. The week is filled with activities and culminates in the Easter Services. Every business does something. Games, prizes, bake sales, races, we do it all. Oh, and a bush dance kicks it all off."

"Sounds like fun. I take it you head up the bake sale?"

She swept a grand gesture to the pie fridge. "Come Easter, that fridge will be fuller than you've ever seen it."

"Well, let me know what I can do to help."

"Absolutely. An extra pair of hands is always, well, handy. You could help with setting up the marquee for the dance. Lucas oversees that."

"Sure. I'll let him know I'm up for whatever he needs."

Aunt Charlotte eyed him sideways. "You know, it's not unheard of to bring a date to the dance. Do you have a girl back in Sydney?"

He chuckled. It was bound to be only a matter of time before his aunt enquired about his love life. "I can't say I do. But I was kind of hoping *you'd* be my date."

"I'd be honoured to have such a strapping young escort, but I won't be offended if you find a lady you'd like to invite between now and then."

"I somehow doubt I will, but I'll let you know." He drained his coffee and slid off the stool. "I'd better get over to the café. Sarah's asked me to update the sockets and fixtures and make sure they're up to code."

Aunt Charlotte clicked her tongue. "This is your day off. You shouldn't be filling it up with more work."

"I'm happy to have the jobs to do. The tasks at the café will be as simple as the ones I did for you this morning, so I'll take the rest of the afternoon off. Happy?"

She pulled a pouty face. "I guess so."

He was about to turn away when she waved her hands. "Oh, could you take something to Willow? She works there, you know."

The girl with the long blonde hair and sad smile. "What would you like me to take?"

His aunt scurried to the refrigerator and produced a cupcake with a beautifully crafted frosted heart. With utmost care, she slid it into a petite pink box before handing it to him. "A treat for her. That girl's had a rough time lately."

His brows lowered. "I'm sorry to hear that. She seems like a nice woman."

Aunt Charlotte crossed her arms, tutted. "That she is. She didn't deserve what happened."

"Oh?" Some might disagree, but Aunt Charlotte never was one to gossip. Still, it couldn't hurt to pry.

"No." She harrumphed. "I've said too much already."

"Come on." He wagged a finger. "You can't leave me hanging."

"Oh, all right, then." She waved him closer and lowered her voice. "She fell in love with a man who proved to be no good. They seemed so well suited—everyone thought so. But after only a month of marriage, he left her for an old flame."

His body jolted. What? "That's shocking."

"It is. The poor girl. She was devastated. Still is. Willow's the most respectable and loyal young woman I know. I don't know how any man could live with himself after treating her like that."

His chest tightened. Though Mum and Dad had been married for years before she discovered his unfaithfulness, Declan had some idea of the pain Willow would be suffering since he'd witnessed it. "That's heartbreaking."

Aunt Charlotte nodded to the cupcake. "It's not much, but I do what I can to remind her I care."

"Thoughtful of you. I'm sure Willow will appreciate it. It looks delicious."

"I'll bring one home for you tonight." She pinched his cheek as if he were a child.

His chest warmed. "Sounds good. See you this evening."

IT HAD BEEN a steady morning at The Coffee Bean Café, but not crazy. Still, Willow felt as exhausted as she did on the busiest of days. No surprise. All anyone could talk about was the upcoming Extravaganza.

Normally, excitement over the annual event would have invigorated her, but memories of last Easter, when she'd struggled to get out of bed, played in her mind like a bad movie. The last thing she wanted to think about was the Extravaganza, as wonderful as the event was.

Swiping a cloth over the espresso machine, she exhaled as she leaned against the counter, taking a much-needed breather from social interaction, and glanced at the clock. Two more hours. Just two.

She drained the last of her morning coffee that had long since gone cold, barely tasting it. She hated feeling like every day she had to fight to make it through. Perhaps things would be easier once Easter was over. The first round of annual events after a heartbreak were the worst, right?

She set her empty cup in the sink as the bell over the door jangled. Turning, she blinked, taken off guard by Declan's arresting smile and the warmth in his dark eyes. "Hello. What can I get you?"

"As great as it smells in here, I haven't come for coffee. Sarah asked me to check the electrical sockets and fixtures to make sure they're up to code."

"Oh. She didn't mention that."

"Sorry. Is it a bad time? She said there's usually a lull around now, so I wouldn't be in your way...?"

Shaking her head, Willow invited him behind the counter with a wave of her hand. It was perfect timing. She just hadn't expected him, and seeing him made her feel oddly out of sorts. "No, it's all right. Do what you need to."

As he headed to the electrical box, she cringed at her drab mood. He must think her a complete killjoy. Still, she couldn't seem to muster any enthusiasm. Besides, he wasn't here to talk, so no need to be chatty.

Pausing, he produced a small box from his bag. "I almost forgot. Charlotte sent this over for you."

"Oh. That was nice of her." Accepting the box, Willow opened it. The cake was gorgeous, but unbidden tears burned her eyes. She blinked them away. "I–I guess she's getting ready for the Extravaganza, too."

"Yes. It seems quite an affair." He turned back to the electrical box.

"It is." She should force some enthusiasm, but what did it matter? She was tired of pretending.

"Does the café do anything special for it?"

She continued cleaning the machine. "Sarah has a coffee and treat stand in the middle of town. I'm sure she'll involve me with that."

His gaze remained fixed on his work at the fuse box. "Not much in the spirit, are you?"

She chuckled. "Not much."

"But it's at Easter, right? The perfect opportunity to draw people's attention to the Cross and the gospel message."

Ouch. He had a point. She traced a smudge on the machine, making it worse. "The services are packed."

"That's great, then."

"There are so many lonely, needy people out there."

"There certainly are."

Something in his voice suggested he might be one of them, although she had no idea how. A guy like him wouldn't have any trouble attracting friends. Especially ones of the female variety.

As if on cue, Lizzy entered, her eyes lighting up at the sight of him. She leaned over the counter to get as close as possible without crossing the customer threshold. "Well, hi there, Declan."

Amused, Willow stood back. Lizzy must've forgotten she'd come for coffee.

"Hi." Declan's greeting was polite. Not warm, but not cold, either. Neutral. "Lizzy, right?"

Her smile almost stretched off her face. "That's right. What are you doing here today?"

"Completing a couple of odd jobs for Sarah."

Lizzy rolled her eyes. "Electrical tasks can hardly be reduced to 'odd jobs.' We're lucky to have an electrician like you around."

Willow might throw up.

"Thanks." He swung his gaze to her. "I'm going to work on the light sockets now. I want to ensure they're all protected by Arc Fault Circuit Interrupters."

Whatever *they* were. She gave a nod. "Feel free to do whatever you need to."

"Are you going to the bush dance?" Lizzy leaned further over the counter, still making no move to place a drink order.

"From what I gather, it'd be hard to avoid." Declan knelt to inspect the socket nearest the espresso machine.

"Everyone goes. It's a great chance to socialise. I'll look forward to seeing you there."

Enough was enough. "Lizzy, can I get you a drink?"

"Oh, yeah. A chai tea latte, thanks."

Lizzy resumed her chat with Declan the moment she finished paying. Willow made the latte and headed into the back room to check on supplies. She had no interest in competing with Lizzy or any other woman for the newcomer's attention. Getting through the hour and a half left of this shift —and then Easter—was challenging enough.

Although he *was* cute.

But she wasn't going there.

No way.

CHAPTER

SEVEN

Declan had only been in Water's Edge two weeks, but the city he'd grown up in already seemed loud and impersonal after the serenity of small-town living.

Although he'd promised to visit Mum, he was hoping to make it a quick one, just long enough to keep her happy and check on her. He'd left Water's Edge after an early morning swim and breakfast at The Coffee Bean Café. He'd half hoped Willow would be working, but instead, a waitress he didn't know served him.

The traffic had been heavy coming towards him with everyone going to the beach. Who'd be going to the city on a day like today? Blue skies, warm temperatures. Perfect swimming weather. But no, he was headed to hot and sticky.

He shouldn't be bitter about spending his Saturday with

Mum. No one else would visit after she told them not to bother. So it was up to him and him alone.

Who'd be an only child?

Even the church folk had stopped dropping by. Who could blame them? She was the most negative person he knew. If she wasn't his mother, he wouldn't bother either.

But no, that wasn't true. She was depressed and hurt. She needed help but refused to see anyone. How she did her job, he wasn't sure. Maybe she put on a happy face for her customers. She wouldn't sell anything if she didn't. Who'd buy a holiday package from a Debby Downer?

That irked. If she could put on a happy face for her customers, why couldn't she do it for him?

But would he want that? No, he'd rather she was honest with him, even if her negativity drove him nuts.

Pulling into the driveway of her double-story brick cul-de-sac home near the university, he steeled himself. And prayed.

Lord, give me an added dose of patience today. I'll need it to handle this visit. Help me to show love to my mum, even if she puts me down. Help me to lift her out of this pit she's in. Give me the words to encourage her to reach out to You. In Jesus' name, I pray. Amen.

The grass was brown and dry. She hadn't watered it. At least he wouldn't have to cut it. And the garbage bins were still out. Collection day had come and gone five days ago.

Climbing out of his ute, he dragged the bins to their spot beside the garage.

He got it. Nobody liked doing the bins, but she'd promised to stay on top of things.

The whole place was a mess. Well, that gave him something to do other than sitting and making small talk.

The front door was closed. He pulled out his key and opened it. "Mum. It's me. Where are you?"

He closed the door behind him. She couldn't still be asleep, could she? Not at almost eleven. He tiptoed to her bedroom. Pushed the door open.

His heartbeat thudded. "Mum..."

He hurried to her. Lifted her off the floor. Settled her on the bed.

Her eyelids flickered. "Ah... Declan. About time."

He stifled a groan. "How are you, Mum?"

She shuffled up the bed and leaned against the pillows. "I've been better."

"How much did you drink last night?"

"None of your business."

"I think it is. You promised you wouldn't drink."

"I lied."

"I can see that. I'll make you some coffee." He hesitated and touched her cheek. Her greying hair was unruly, and her eyes bleary. "Did you go to work this week?"

She crossed her arms. "None of your business."

"I take that as a no." He drew a long breath. What was he to do?

Her eyes narrowed. "What happened to that coffee?"

He counted to ten. Smiled. "Coming right up."

In the kitchen, he moved dirty dishes and utensils to make room on the counter for two clean mugs he found at the back of the cupboard. While waiting for the kettle to boil, he ran water into the sink and washed the dishes. The dishwasher was full but hadn't been on. A putrid odour oozed from it. A week's worth of dirty dishes, no doubt. Grabbing a dishwasher tablet, he tossed it in and turned the machine on.

He threw a slice of stale bread into the toaster, poured boiling water into the mugs, and looked in the fridge for milk. Just enough for one. Great. He'd be having his black.

"Declan. Where's my coffee?"

Lord, give me patience. "It's coming, Mum."

"So's Christmas."

Yes, it was. "I'm on my way."

He unearthed a plate, buttered the toast and spread it with marmalade, set the plate and mugs on a tray, and carried it all to her room.

"Took your time, didn't you?"

He pinned her with his gaze. How much more could he take? Seriously? "I made some toast."

She cast her gaze to the plate as he set it on a bed tray and handed it to her. "I would have preferred honey."

He gritted his teeth. "I can make another piece if you like."

She waved him off. "Don't bother. I'm not hungry, anyway."

He perched on the edge of the bed. Sipped his coffee. Studied her. Despite the dark circles under her brown eyes, she was still an attractive woman. Or could be. Her hair, thick, wavy, and grey, reached her shoulders. When Dad was around, she'd dyed it blonde. Now, she didn't bother.

When he left, she'd stopped bothering with everything.

"So, would you like to go for a drive? We could go to Katoomba. Have lunch up there. Or we could go to the beach. Or I could take you shopping. Whatever you want."

"I don't know why you bother asking. You know I won't go anywhere."

"One day, I'm hoping you will."

"Yeah, well. I have no interest. You know that. I don't see the point."

"You'd feel a whole lot better if you made even a tiny effort."

Her shoulders drooped. "I don't have the energy."

"Because you're not eating. You're fading away." So much so that he was growing concerned. But how did you force a grown woman to eat?

Drawing a long breath, he prayed silently for her. Only God could reach deep inside her heart and heal her emotional wounds.

But instead of turning to Him when Dad left, she blamed Him.

If only she'd opened her eyes, she would've seen he left because she wasn't a nice person to be around anymore.

Declan had seen it happening. The barbed comments she gave Dad when he arrived home a few minutes late. The cold shoulder at the dinner table. He wasn't sure what had caused it. Perhaps Dad had been unfaithful. Declan had been only a kid when it started and wasn't privy to such things. All he could do was look on as his parents' marriage imploded. He always knew one day Dad would leave.

And now, Declan must pick up the pieces.

He inhaled. "Okay. We can stay home, watch a movie, chat. Whatever you want."

A sheen came over her eyes. "You're a good boy, Declan. I'm sorry for not being better company."

His brow lifted. Wow. A compliment. She wasn't all bad.

He gave her a warm smile. "It's okay, Mum. I'm happy to be here."

And so, the day passed.

Guilt plagued him when, midafternoon, he made moves to leave. He should stay. But how could he? She'd pull them both down.

She'd brushed her hair and eaten some soup, but still wore her dressing gown. She'd stay in it all weekend, no doubt. Maybe she'd go to work on Monday. Maybe she wouldn't. How was it she still had a job?

"I'll come back soon, Mum, but call if you need anything."

"I'm sure you've got better things to do than visit me."

Yeah. But how could he not come?

Crossing the floor, he reached down and hugged her. "I'll come. Okay?"

She lifted her gaze and gave the tiniest of smiles.

"Take care. Love you." He kissed the top of her head and walked out the door.

Heaviness weighed on him as he headed to his ute. She

stood on the verandah, hugging her dressing gown around her slight frame, and waved as he drove off.

How much longer, Lord? How much longer?

Releasing a heavy breath, he joined the traffic heading south, put his foot down, and turned the radio up. At Water's Edge, he drove straight to the beach. Aunt Charlotte was hosting a dinner party with friends, so he had no need to rush home. A swim would help clear his head.

He found a park and climbed out, stretched. After grabbing his towel, he jogged down the path and onto the warm sand. In the late afternoon sunshine, the water glinted like a jewel.

Between the flags, children laughed as their parents helped them catch wave after wave into the shore. Once upon a time, he and Dad did that.

Dad... Sighing, Declan picked up his pace. He didn't love jogging, but pounding the hard sand was cathartic after a visit with Mum.

She hated that he still saw Dad. Dad had moved to a northern suburb of Sydney with Rosemary and her two teenage children. Seeing him with a new, ready-made family was weird. Rosemary always welcomed him, but Declan felt he was intruding. He preferred to meet Dad at a neutral venue, like a café or a restaurant. Sometimes, they caught a movie together. He refrained from telling Mum about their catch-ups unless she asked, and when she did, he didn't give details. No use upsetting her further.

He was building up a sweat when a woman jogged

towards him, arms pumping, long blonde ponytail swinging from side to side with each step.

Willow? His eyes narrowed.

Yes, it was her. He slowed, and their gazes connected.

She paused, stopped, and tucked wisps of hair behind her ear. The slightest smile curved her lips before she ducked her head. "Hey."

Although panting, he managed a reply. "Hey, yourself. Nice day for a jog."

"Yes. Do you do this often?"

He shook his head. "Nope. Do you?"

Her chest heaved. Black bike pants and a pink crop top showed off her trim figure. She was a looker, for sure. "I've started to. I needed to do something different."

Yep. He got that. If only Mum would come to that conclusion.

"Same here. I've just come back from visiting my mother and needed to clear my head."

The ponytail flipped over her shoulder as she tilted her head. "Where does she live?"

"Sydney. Near the uni. Dad used to lecture there."

"Oh. Amelia and I go to USS. Is that the one?"

A seagull swooped overhead, his shadow chasing the incoming waves. Declan breathed deeply, savouring the tangy salt-scented air. "He lectured in Physics."

A toss of her head sent her ponytail down her back as her smile widened and the beginnings of a dimple winked at him.

"I don't know anything about Physics. I'm studying fashion, and Amelia's doing nursing."

Fashion, huh? Made sense.

They began strolling along the water's edge towards the flagged swimming stretch.

"Are you enjoying your studies?"

She released a heavy breath and slid her hand around the back of her neck. "I was."

His brows came together. "But not now?"

She shrugged. "Things changed."

Man, could he relate to that.

She scuffled her bare feet in the wet sand, splashing up water. "Since Charlotte's your aunt, I'm guessing you know my story."

Oops. He held his hands up. "Sorry. She mentioned it the other day."

"I figured. It's okay. You would've found out. No one has any secrets for long in Water's Edge." Her eyes were as blue as the ocean, but like his mother's, they carried hurt.

He almost reached to touch her hand. Instead, he softened his voice. "It must have been awful."

She scuffled her feet again, digging her toes into the wet sand. "I'm trying to move forward."

"But it's not easy?"

She bent down and picked up a pipi. "I take one day at a time. That's all I can do."

At her honesty, an ache tore through his heart. "I understand. My mum's still struggling after my dad left two years ago."

"For someone else?"

He nodded. "It destroyed her. I'm praying for a breakthrough. Something has to happen soon."

Her head jerked up, guileless blue eyes fixing on him. "She's that bad?"

The breeze kicked wisps of hair into those eyes. His fingers twitched to brush them away. "Sadly, yes. I've lived with her for the past two years, but I needed a break. That's why I'm here."

"You couldn't have come to a better place. And Charlotte adores you."

"She's a good egg."

They both chuckled as a rogue wave caught them unawares and water splashed their knees.

He gripped her elbow to steady her. "I–I guess you don't remember me staying with her when I was a kid?"

Willow frowned. "Hmm... I think I do. You hung with the Markopoulos boys."

"Yeah, that was them. Nikolas and Dion."

"The family moved away years ago."

"I remember coming one year, and they were gone. Aunt Charlotte said they went back to Greece."

The breeze was stronger now, slapping those tendrils of escaping hair around her eyes. With both hands, she pinned it down. "Why did you stop coming?"

His shoulders drooped, the repressive weight returning.

"Things weren't great at home, and Mum needed me."

"You're obviously a good son."

Everyone but Mum thought so. No, not true. She'd admitted it last time, hadn't she? "I try to be, but I fear I fail."

"You're too hard on yourself. Sometimes people need space to figure things out on their own."

Good point. "You're speaking from personal experience."

Her eyes dimmed before she ducked her head again. "It doesn't matter how many people you go to for help—nothing changes until you decide to let go of the bitterness and move on. Not even God can force a person to do that."

"So, have you let go of the bitterness?"

She drew in a deep breath, blinking rapidly as if fighting emotion. "I'm–I'm working on it."

More than he could say about his mum. Maybe one day Willow could talk to her.

They reached the flagged area. "Care for a swim?"

The beginnings of a smile flashed again, making him feel as if he'd won something precious even as she backed out of the water towards the dry sand. "I need to get back. I've got an assignment to do."

"Well, it's been nice talking with you."

That slight smile warmed. "Yes. It was."

"See you in church?"

She gave a nod. "I'll be there."

"*I'll* look forward to it."

Her pretty blue eyes clouded over, and he realised what he'd done. He wasn't trying to come onto her, but she probably thought he was. He'd sounded way too enthusiastic. What a goose.

She jogged back to the car park, and he flopped onto his towel. A swim didn't seem quite so appealing now.

WILLOW STRUGGLED to focus that night. How could she work on equations when all she could think about was Declan and their beach encounter?

Since Jason, she'd felt not the smallest spark of interest towards anyone. So how was it that she'd felt something?

But could she ever trust her feelings again? She'd listened to her heart once before—yeah, look how that ended.

Closing her laptop, she went to the fridge, grabbed a Coke, and stepped onto the porch. Light clouds partially covered the moon, and the gentle breeze made her shiver.

They'd shared an enjoyable and meaningful conversation. That was all. No reason to start imagining a special connection.

But something deep inside had stirred. It was more than a superficial attraction. They *had* connected. She was sure of it. He was a decent man who cared for his mother. Who understood Willow's struggles.

But she wasn't ready for anything more than friendship. She didn't trust herself. She *had* to stop thinking about him. The only way was to focus on this assignment and banish every other thought. She could do that. She had to. But equations? Who'd have thought she'd have to study equations in a fashion design course? Crazy.

With her head clear and her thoughts under control, she returned to tackle her assignment.

At church the following day, she steered clear of him, which wasn't difficult since Lizzy and another of her friends monopolised him. Willow also tried to ignore the spark of jealousy burning inside her.

CHAPTER
EIGHT

L ater that week, as Declan made his way inside the Youth Centre, children's playful shrieks followed him. When he set foot in the front room, a small person attacked his legs.

Ezekiel threw his head back and looked straight up. "Sorry, Mr. Ross."

Declan couldn't help chuckling. "It's all right, Ezekiel. Where are you headed in such a hurry?"

"The basketball tournament. Do you wanna come? You can be on my team!" He jittered from foot to foot, breathless.

Declan ruffled his hair. "I wish I could. But I've just stopped by to check on a few things, and then I'm off to Sydney for the day. Next time, okay?"

Ezekiel barely managed a nod before he raced away.

Declan's smile lingered as he approached the work-in-progress area in the recreation room. Lucas and Amelia were already there, which he'd expected.

But Willow? That was a surprise. A nice one, though.

Since he'd bumped into her on the beach, he'd only seen her at church, but he'd gotten the impression she'd avoided him.

His fault, of course.

He'd thought of dropping into the café, but he'd only make things worse if she thought he was chasing her. He wasn't. But if she *was* ready, he'd be interested in pursuing a friendship. Or more.

She was gorgeous, but her resilience impressed him more. Despite what she'd been through, she appeared to be growing stronger. Moving forward. More than he could say for his mum.

He gave her a nod as their gazes met. She didn't turn away. That was something.

It had been a long time since he'd felt anything for a woman. The few he'd dated in Sydney had been shallow, and he'd grown bored and decided to wait until God brought the right girl into his life.

Could it be Willow? His heart warmed.

He greeted the group, relieved his voice sounded normal despite the flutter in his chest. Then he cleared his throat and spoke to Lucas. "Did the supplies come in?"

Lucas tapped a cardboard box with the toe of his boot. "Sure did. You'll be all set for next week. You're doing a great job here, mate."

"Thanks. Glad you're happy."

"We're more than happy." Seated beside Lucas, Amelia smiled. But her face seemed strained, and an odd colour tinted it. Green?

He didn't know much about pregnancies, but she seemed too slight to be carrying a baby. "Are you okay?"

Her smile wavered. "Just a little extra morning sickness today."

"Oh."

She shuffled in her chair. "I thought I'd be okay to drive to uni with Willow, but the thought of sitting in a car makes me feel worse." She winced and waved to Willow. "Sorry. Nothing personal."

Willow squeezed her hand. "Don't worry about it. Get some rest, okay?"

Declan swallowed the lump in his throat. Could he suggest *they* travel to the city together since Amelia wasn't going? He was heading up there.... It made sense. But what would Willow think?

Only one way to find out.

He cleared his throat again. Faced her. "I'm headed to town. I thought I'd visit Mum again since I have the day off. Would you like to go together and save on fuel?" He held his breath, half-expecting her to decline.

The moments she took to reply seemed an eternity. "It makes sense." She glanced at her watch. "But we'll need to get going if I'm to make it on time."

"No problem. I'm ready to leave."

She rubbed Amelia's shoulder. "Let me know if I can bring anything back for you."

"I will. Thanks."

Willow grabbed her bag and followed him to his ute. On the outside court, the basketball tournament was in full swing. He waved to Ezekiel, then scooted ahead, and opened the passenger door. Once she'd climbed in and he'd closed the door, he rounded the ute and slid onto his seat.

"Sorry for the mess." He picked up an empty Coke can and pie bag and stuffed them under his seat. Aunt Charlotte would be horrified to discover he'd supplemented her healthy breakfast with a pie and soft drink, but she'd never find out if he could help it.

"No worries." Shrugging it off, Willow waved to the children as he drove out of the car park, and then she faced the front and folded her hands in her lap.

His fingers tapped the steering wheel as he waited to enter the main highway to Sydney. The slower, more picturesque coastal road would've been a nicer drive. But she was on a schedule, so the highway it was.

Keenly aware of her sitting beside him, he snuck a sideways glance. At least today, she was wearing jeans and a button-up shirt. Her perfume floated in the air—a fresh and light citrus scent.

"I hope you don't mind having me for a carpool buddy. I know nothing can replace girl-talk."

"It's fine." She cinched her loose ponytail tighter. "Thanks for the ride. I don't mind the drive, but going together makes sense."

An awkward silence hung between them. Finally, since she'd seemed happy to speak on the beach, he asked how she was doing. After all, they'd already passed the small-talk stage, so why not ditch it?

She crossed her arms. "Still one day at a time, although I can see light at the end of the tunnel."

He faced her. "That's great."

"I blamed God, you know."

Ouch. He knew all about that. "Really?"

"I'd believed Jason was the one chosen for me, and so when he left, I struggled to understand how it had gone so wrong. Why God didn't stop him from leaving."

"I can see how you'd think that."

"I still don't understand, but it's becoming clearer. I jumped in too quickly. Amelia and Lucas had just married when he arrived in town, and I was feeling left behind. We clicked, and I assumed it was a God thing. Maybe it was, but Jason wasn't honest with me. He told me he was over his previous girlfriend, but he wasn't. I feel so stupid. I should have seen that he married me on the rebound. But I was so ready to be loved that I ignored the signs." She sniffed. "I'm sorry. I didn't mean to lose it in front of you."

Without thinking, he reached out and squeezed her hand. "It's okay. I appreciate you sharing."

A moment passed as their gazes held before he withdrew his hand, placed it on the wheel, and focused on the road.

"You're a good listener."

"You think so?"

She nodded. "But now, it's your turn. Tell me about you."

Oh. He freed one hand from the wheel and rubbed along his jaw. "What do you want to know?"

"Whatever you want to tell me."

"Okay..." He tapped the wheel. "Well, I'm an only child. I grew up in Sydney, and my dad's a lecturer. My mum works part-time as a travel agent, although I don't know how she does her job."

"Maybe it's what keeps her sane."

"Yeah, maybe." Sane wasn't a word he'd use for her, though.

"Okay. What else?"

"I used to stay with Aunt Charlotte during the holidays."

"Was that a bit strange?"

"Not really. Mum and Dad fought a lot, and I was glad to get away. Aunt Charlotte spoiled me."

Willow chuckled. "She spoils everyone."

"I've seen that in action these past few weeks."

"So, that's your childhood. How did you become a Christian?"

"Again, Aunt Charlotte. The way she talked about God made so much sense that, when she asked me one night if I'd like to give my life to Jesus, I said yes."

"And you've never strayed?"

"I wouldn't say that. When I left school, I went travelling with a mate, and he led me astray. Or I led him. One or the other. We parted ways eventually, and I got my life back on track."

"Where did you go?"

"Oh, the usual haunts. Bali, Thailand, Cambodia, Vietnam, India, Nepal."

She gave a little gasp. "Wow. Did you ride an elephant?"

"Sure did. Some of the places we went to were amazing. Ankor Wat, the Taj Mahal, Kathmandu." He twisted his grip on the steering wheel, restless as memories floated back.

"I've never been out of Australia."

"Would you like to travel?"

A small breath escaped her. "Jason and I talked about going to New Zealand. But that never happened."

Sadness returned to her voice, tightening a cord around his heart. "Maybe you could still go?"

Was that a quick headshake or a shudder? "Not on my own."

"You've got friends. Couldn't you go with one of them?"

"I'd only go with Amelia, but now she's married and having a baby."

"Well, you never know what's around the corner."

"I guess you're right." She shifted in her seat, tucking a shoulder against the backrest as she faced him, and their gazes held.

He swallowed hard. *Lord, don't let me spoil this.*

When he smiled at her, she returned it. Hope welled inside him. Maybe he hadn't blown it after all.

He slowed for a red light. With how quickly time had

passed, they were almost there. She gave him directions and, as she got out, thanked him for sharing.

He promised to pick her up at three.

Five hours with Mum. His shoulders slumped, but when Willow turned and waved, her smile buoyed him. At least he had something to look forward to.

Another ninety minutes with Willow.

Sweet.

LATE THE FOLLOWING MORNING, Willow called in on Amelia. Amelia was in bed, surrounded by throw blankets, pillows, and home-improvement and motherhood magazines. Her eyelids were drooping, but she brightened as Willow walked in.

"Hey."

"Hey yourself." Willow settled on the edge of the bed. "How are you feeling?"

Amelia shrugged. "Tired, queasy, but it's nothing serious. I feel silly being such a bother."

Willow squeezed her hand. "You could never be a bother. The little person inside you is simply reminding us he or she is there and you need to take it easy."

Amelia rubbed her stomach, her smile widening. "It's still hard to believe it's happening. I don't like missing classes and not being able to work. But when I think of our little baby and how blessed we are, I get a warm feeling inside, and I feel so grateful."

"As you should. No doubt Dr. Turner's missing you, but he'd be the first to insist you get the rest you need."

Amelia let out a low huff. "I know it's important. But I feel so detached from everything already, and this is only the second day." She adjusted her position in the bed. "Hopefully, I'll feel better by tomorrow."

"I'm sure you will."

"Oh, he called and told me Courtney came in for a follow-up appointment and is doing well."

"That's good to hear." Willow opened the Thermos containing the chicken soup she'd made, poured some into a cup, and handed it to Amelia.

She took the soup but made no move to taste it. "She's still not sure what she'll do once the baby's born. It's so heart-breaking. Since her grandfather is anything but helpful, she has no support apart from Doc and me. When I'm not laid up in bed, that is."

"That's so sad," Willow murmured. "She shouldn't be facing this on her own. Do we know anything about the father?"

"She refuses to talk about him."

Willow pursed her lips. "Men. Are there any good ones out there?"

Amelia's brow lifted. "Lucas. Declan."

At Declan's name, Willow's pulse accelerated. She lowered

her gaze and cleared her throat as her cheeks warmed. "I guess there are some."

Moments passed before she nudged Amelia's arm. "Hey, eat your soup. I slaved over a hot stove to make it for you."

Amelia sniffed the cup, then tested a sip. "Mmm, that's good." She drank some more. "Thanks for bringing my coursework. Most of it's online, but this extra stuff helps with my assignments. It's frustrating not going to prac, though."

"I'm sure the hospital will accommodate you when you feel better."

"I hope so. I'd hate to get so far behind I can't graduate." She braved another sip. "So, how was carpooling with Declan?"

"It was fine."

"Just fine, huh?"

"Yes." Willow fiddled with her hoop earring.

"Okay."

She looked up. Narrowed her eyes. "What?"

"Come on." Amelia went into singsong. "Youuuu liiiike hiiiimmmm."

Heat rushed to Willow's cheeks. What had Amelia seen? Declan was a nice guy, and maybe she was attracted to him. But she was in no way ready for another relationship. She crossed her arms. "Not in the way you mean."

Seeming to focus on the soup, Amelia swirled the cup as if making sure no goodies remained at the bottom. "Are you sure?"

"After what I've been through, I'm not about to jump into another relationship, even if I do like the guy."

"See. You admit it."

Humph... "He's easygoing, and we chatted the whole way. Happy?"

"Uh-huh." Amelia angled her head. "And?"

"We took the long way home."

Amelia slurped the last of the soup. "And how did that go?"

Warmth surged through Willow, and she grinned. "It was nice."

"See."

"See what?"

Setting the empty soup cup aside, Amelia leaned towards Willow and clasped her hand. "Don't let what happened in the past interfere with the blessings God's sending your way now. Embrace those blessings. Declan's a good man. And he likes you. I saw it yesterday morning when he offered to carpool. You don't know what might happen if you get to know him."

Amelia might be right. Willow shouldn't let Jason and Darlene's behaviour rob her of God's future blessings, but was she ready to open her heart to love again? Or even friendship? She released a heavy breath. Although she doubted Declan would ever cast her aside like Jason did, she didn't know him. Not really.

But that didn't mean she *couldn't* get to know him.

Her heart quickened.

Could she learn to love again?

Could she risk her heart once more?

A tiny smile parted her lips. "Thanks. I'll think on that. But hey, you need to eat more than soup. You're eating for two, don't forget."

Amelia rolled her eyes. "How could I forget when I feel so ill?"

Willow squeezed her hand. "Let me pray for you?"

At Amelia's grateful nod, Willow closed her eyes. Took a slow breath. She might be praying for Amelia, but they both needed a touch from the Lord.

"Heavenly Father, we come before You with gratitude for this new life Amelia is carrying. Bless this dear little one as he or she grows inside Amelia's womb, and give Amelia strength to get through this time of sickness. Let her know Your peace and comfort. Bless her and Lucas as they anticipate the safe arrival of this little bundle."

Willow swallowed hard. "And, Lord, please help me let go of the bitterness I still feel towards Jason. Help me to trust You with my future and to know that You have something better planned for me. We ask these things in Jesus' precious name. Amen."

CHAPTER
NINE

Declan stared at his coffee cup, playing absently with the silverware beside it. It had been three days since he and Willow carpooled to Sydney, and he hadn't seen her since. Not even at church. Was she avoiding him again?

"You look far away." Aunt Charlotte braced a hip against his table. Deep in thought, he hadn't heard her approach.

He shrugged and wrapped his hands around the cup. "I was in my own little world."

She motioned to his empty pie plate. "How was the apple rhubarb?"

He patted his stomach. "Delicious."

"Can I get you anything else? More coffee?"

"No, I'm fine, but thank you."

She eyed him before sliding into the booth across from him. "A penny for your thoughts?"

He exhaled and lifted his gaze to hers. May as well tell her. She'd keep digging until he did. "I've developed a fondness for Willow, and I'm not sure what to do about it."

"Oh my giddy aunt! I'd prayed that would happen."

"You didn't."

She slapped the table. "I did. You two would be perfect for each other."

Maybe, but... "She's not ready for another relationship."

"No, but nothing's wrong with friendship. It's better to take it slowly, anyway." She reached over and patted his hand. "Being her friend is a great start."

She was right. He could be Willow's friend, and if it developed into something more in the future, all the better. But if it didn't? He'd have to take his chances.

He drained the last of the coffee and pushed to his feet, bending over to kiss his aunt's cheek. "Thanks for the advice and for the pie. See you tonight." With that, he made his way out of the diner, his thoughts already set on the job waiting for him at the Youth Centre. And how to develop a friendship with a certain young lady.

WILLOW FLOPPED her head against the pillow, switching from her side to her back again as someone's headlights played across her ceiling, the crisscross of the half-open vertical blinds casting shadows like rungs on a baby's cot. What would it feel like to be expecting like Amelia, to have the future opening up before her?

Groan. Why was she thinking like this? She squeezed her eyes shut and willed her breathing to steady. Unlikely she'd sleep, but maybe...

WILLOW HELD up the seafoam-green linen napkin for Jason's approval. "What do you think?"

He tipped his head. "You know, I never would've thought of using that as an accent colour, but I like it."

"Done." She beamed, jotting down the colour on the notepad containing the wedding details, then glanced around the wedding store. "We've got just about everything planned for the reception. We can turn our list in to the front desk now so they can get it all together for us."

He came forward, love in his eyes as he took her in his arms and placed a tender kiss on her forehead. "I know you were excited to have help from wedding professionals here in the shop, but you didn't need any assistance. Thanks to your designer's eye, everything will be perfectly coordinated."

She smiled again as warmth spread through her. How she loved this man. "Thank you, hon. It's so much fun."

As he wagged a finger, his expression turned playful. "And you're going to have a lot more of it. First, there'll be the house to decorate and then the nursery...."

Her eyes widened, her heart hammering in her chest. Nursery. Unbelievable! In a matter of weeks, she'd be married to this man standing before her—this handsome, caring man who was eager to share his life with her.

His brows arched. "Too soon to talk about kids?"

She rose on tiptoes to kiss his cheek. "Never. I can't wait to start a family with you."

She would have said more, but he silenced her with a kiss.

...

WILLOW'S EYELIDS SNAPPED OPEN. She stared up at the dark ceiling, emptiness enveloping her as she pulled herself from her dreamland haze. Sitting up, she winced at the glare from the clock blinking on the bedside table. Three a.m.

Groaning, she dropped back against her pillows, willing herself to sleep. After tossing and turning, she gave up, wriggled her feet into slippers, and tugged on a bathrobe. Then she padded out into the kitchen. She warmed a cup of milk, sprinkling cinnamon over the top before returning to her room. Settling down, she sipped the milk and prayed silently.

But the queasiness caused by her vivid dream of Jason mingled sickeningly with the milk she soon set aside. Despite the nagging feeling telling her not to, she walked back out to the living room. At the bookshelf, she paused, exhaled, and reached for the ornate wooden box on the highest shelf.

Seated on the overstuffed blue velvet couch, she traced her fingers along the box's edges before lifting the lid. Just as she'd expected, a million memories of Jason seared her as she sifted through the contents. Movie ticket stubs, handwritten notes, pictures taken in mall photo booths, and dozens of other mementos swam before her moist eyes. When her eyes became too blurred to see the items, his face haunted her.

"Jason, how could you?" Gasping, she pressed a hand to her mouth.

She should have gotten rid of the box a long time ago. It only revived memories and questions. She fingered the note he'd written one morning while she was still in bed. Had he loved her at all? Was he thinking of his ex the entire time they were together, even when they were engaged and married?

Heat coursing through her, she flung the box from her lap. It thudded on the floor, the contents spilling. She hugged her arms around her middle, panting and rocking back and forth as a fresh onslaught of tears threatened.

She would have succumbed to the pain if an unusual buzzing hadn't caught her attention.

Swiping the tears from her cheeks, she pushed to her feet and shuffled to the kitchen. She followed the sound to the electrical box in the pantry, then, frowning, unclicked the latch. With the door open, the buzzing intensified. She groaned. She may not know about electrical matters, but even she knew this wasn't something one should leave unattended.

She grabbed her phone from the kitchen counter and called Dad.

Not surprising, when he answered, he sounded half-asleep.

"Sorry to wake you, Dad, but there's a problem." When she explained, he agreed to come.

Within minutes, she was back on the couch, one foot idly kicking at the box's scattered contents as she awaited his arrival. She should clean up the mess, but how could she touch one item from it while grief over Jason's betrayal engulfed her afresh?

How *had* it gone so wrong?

By the time the doorbell rang, heat was searing her eyes. Sniffing, she dabbed them as she made her way to the door. Dad would see she was upset, but she could do little about that. She could blame her emotional state on being tired and unable to sleep because of the electrical box, but would he believe her?

She opened the door, and her eyelids flew open. "Declan!" She swiped her hands over her cheeks, cleared her throat. "I–I didn't expect you."

He regarded her, his gaze gentle. "Your dad said you have a suspicious humming coming from your electrical box. He was going to come. But he figured it would need an electrician, so he called me."

Oh. She tried to mask her inner turmoil. "He didn't need to do that. It's four in the morning."

He shrugged. "Emergencies don't wait until it's convenient, and that buzzing qualifies. Can I take a look?"

"Of course. Thank you. The box is in the pantry." She stepped aside, allowing him to enter. As he followed her down the hallway, she tucked her dishevelled hair behind her ears, keenly aware of how frumpy she must appear in her bathrobe and slippers.

Businesslike, he tucked right into examining the box.

Without another word, she retreated to the living room. Dropping onto the couch, she wrapped her arms around herself and stared at the bookshelf.

She and Jason had chosen it together. She remembered the day. He'd come by early that Saturday morning, and they went for breakfast at a new café on the boardwalk down by the sea. Afterwards, he suggested they wander through town and look at the shops. It wasn't his favourite activity, but she enjoyed it. And he loved her so much he just wanted to make her happy.

She'd loved that about him.

He always put her first.

They wandered into the furniture shop. They didn't need many new items since he was moving into her fully furnished house once they were married, but she fell in love with this shelf. It was *so* her, and it matched her oak coffee table. They paid cash for it, and he went back for his ute and took it home that day. She'd filled it with potted plants, books, photos, and candles.

Her eyes burned again. Memories of the life she'd shared with him for such a short time were everywhere. There was no escaping them. Mum said she should move. She might be right.

If they were still married, Jason would've known what to do with this electrical box malfunction. There would have been no need to call Dad. Yet, here she was, living alone. She could have gotten a new housemate, but emotionally drained, she couldn't bear the thought of getting to know someone new.

Besides, Amelia had been the perfect housemate. How would Willow ever find anyone like her again?

Wrapped up in her sadness, she nearly forgot Declan was there until he emerged from the kitchen.

"Found the problem." He stood there, looking so handsome her breath caught. "Looks like a hard short. I replaced your circuit breaker, so you should be all set."

He was talking a different language. She swiped her hands over her damp cheeks again. "Er, okay. Thank you."

He hesitated before making his way to a matching overstuffed chair opposite her. "May I?"

"Sure."

Moments of silence passed before he spoke, his voice gentle. "Are you okay?"

Nodding, she somehow managed a watery smile. "I'm fine. Don't worry about me."

He leaned towards her, his already dark eyes darkening. "The electrical issues worried you that much?"

He must think her pathetic. She waved off his words, cleared her throat. "It wasn't the electrical issues. I mean, it was sort of... Oh, I don't know." Hard as she tried to squelch the tears building behind her eyes, they misted over. A pit formed in her stomach as his gaze swept over the debris on the floor.

"I meant to pick it all up." She scrambled to gather the mementos and shove them back into the box. After setting it on the oak coffee table and settling back onto the couch, she avoided looking at him as long as possible. When she did meet his gaze, open compassion peered back at her.

She shook her head. Shrugged. "I wasn't thinking. I just... threw it."

His gaze settled on the box. "Memories?"

She replied with a nod.

"I'm sorry you've had such a rough night."

Drained, she slumped back against the couch and massaged her temples. "I'm always a mess when you're around."

"You're experiencing human emotions. We all have them."

She rubbed the velvet cushion the wrong way, creating a line in the fabric. "I wish I could get through them and move on, but every time I think I am, they come right back again."

He angled his head. Folded his arms. "When Mum discovered Dad had been unfaithful for years without her knowing, she experienced every emotion possible."

Years. At least she hadn't had that. It had been swift and unexpected. Knocked her for six, but gave her the chance to start again while she was young.

Her throat closed. "I'm so sorry."

"Thanks. I'm amazed how long Dad was able to keep us in the dark. It was a shock when we found out, but Mum felt the most betrayed. Years of the life they'd built together was destroyed, leaving her feeling used and abandoned."

"He left, then?"

Declan nodded. "He did. She still hasn't regained her trust

in men. She hasn't regained trust in anything." He paused before looking her straight in the eyes. "Because of his betrayal, she lost her confidence and enjoyment of everything she used to love."

His words pricked Willow's heart, not only out of compassion for what his mother had suffered but also because they struck a chord of truth in her as well.

Jason's betrayal had stolen so much from her. It wasn't fair.

Declan shuffled in his seat, braced an elbow on his knee, found her gaze. "You're an amazing woman, Willow. It didn't take me long to realise that. I know you've been hurt, but I'd hate to see you lose your passion for life. What Jason did to you isn't a reflection on your value or worth. You have so much to offer people. You're gracious and kind. I've seen it in action."

Willow fanned her face as a shaky laugh jittered loose. "You're going to trigger waterworks again."

Understanding edged his smile, gleamed in his dark eyes. "I didn't intend that, but if tears come, it's all right. Let them out. Crying can be a good release."

"So long as one day they stop." She dabbed her eyes.

"I guess there's that." His eyes twinkled, and his smile crinkled up into a full-on grin.

Wow. Who knew a guy like that could possess such sensitivity? She sat up straighter on the couch. Sure, he *was* amazing, but could she trust her heart to another again?

He ran his hand over his dark hair, her baby-pink curtains

framing him. "I'm here to help, whether it's an electrical emergency or something else. Anything."

"Thank you." With the tension melting from her muscles, her heart warmed further. "I appreciate that."

"You look like you could use a hug." Standing, he opened his arms. "May I?"

A hug. That sounded so nice.

"That would be lovely." She pushed to her feet as he crossed the room.

Stepping into his arms, she rested her head against his chest. "Thank you. For everything."

He rubbed her back and pressed his cheek to hers before pulling back. "Of course. You're a beautiful, special person, Willow. Don't let anything or anyone change that. Deal?"

She chuckled. "Deal."

He held her gaze for another beat before nodding. "I'll let you get some sleep. See you soon."

"For sure. Bye. And thanks again."

After following him to the door, she remained on the porch as his headlights disappeared into the darkness.

A light breeze ruffled her hair. Above, stars sprinkled the sky like fairy dust as the stillness of night brought a sense of peace.

That the God of creation held this finely balanced universe in His hands yet had time for her and her troubles blew her away.

The Lord is near to all who call on Him, to all who call on Him in truth. He fulfills the desires of those who fear Him; He hears their cry and saves them. The Lord watches over all who love Him, but all the wicked He will destroy. My mouth will speak in praise of the Lord. Let every creature praise His holy name for ever and ever.

How could she sleep? But she'd be useless at work if she didn't get some rest.

In bed later, she closed her eyes. Instead of gruesome images of Jason and Darlene, images of Declan overtook her, and she drifted off to sleep with a smile on her face and peace in her heart.

CHAPTER
TEN

"What do you think of putting the banner above the craft table with the kiddos' paper crosses underneath?" Willow held up the colourful banner for her sister-in-law's inspection.

The Youth Centre's recreation room was getting more and more festive each passing minute.

Amelia paused from sorting through a box of craft supplies. "That'd be perfect. I'm sure glad you're here to help me figure out what to do with all these decorations."

Willow waved her off. "You'd be fine. I'm happy to help, though."

Head cocked to one side, Amelia eyed her. "You seem more positive about the festivities."

Hmm. Willow wasn't feeling so down, and it had everything to do with what Declan had said the night he checked her electrical box. With his words strengthening her, she was doing her best to ignore the memories that stung her whenever she let her guard down. "I've reached a place where I might be able to enjoy it."

"Good."

Though her sister-in-law was smiling, there was no missing the strain on her face. "Amelia, are you feeling all right?"

Amelia's forehead crinkled as she hesitated and placed a hand on her stomach. "I'm not sure. I started the day with the usual morning sickness. I figured it would go away, so I came here. The nausea went away, but I still... feel off."

Willow's brow lowered. "Off, how?"

"My stomach doesn't feel quite right, and my head..." Amelia shrugged. "I'm sure it's nothing, just the usual stuff."

That didn't sound right. Willow's heartbeat thudded. Or was her pessimism thinking for her again? "If you say so. But you should take it easy. Have you seen Dr. Turner lately?"

Waving a hand, Amelia laughed. "I see him all the time."

No way was she letting her bestie off that easily. "I mean, for a check-up."

Amelia shook her head. "Trust me, I'm fine. I'll let you know if I'm not."

Still uneasy, Willow had little choice but to return to her placement of the banner. She pulled up a stool and grabbed a handful of thumbtacks. Stepping up, she positioned one side of the banner. "That ought to be high enough. What do you think?" When there was no answer, her gaze flew to her sister-in-law, and her insides twisted.

Amelia's face was ghastly white.

Willow was by her side in a flash.

Amelia clutched her arm and pressed the other to the small of her back.

"It's your back now?" Willow asked.

A sheen of sweat had formed on Amelia's forehead. She nodded, her breathing shallow. Her voice shook when she finally spoke. "I need... to get... clinic."

"Of course." Willow's heart pounded as she helped Amelia to the car.

Not fifteen minutes later, Willow was in the waiting room with nothing to do but pace. She whirled to the front door when Lucas entered, his eyes wide. "Is Amelia all right?"

Stepping forward, she embraced her brother. "I don't know yet. She's with Dr. Turner."

Lucas clung to her. "If anything happens—"

Willow pulled back, looked him straight in the eye. "Don't say that. She's going to be fine. She's in God's hands. Nothing that happens to her is out of His control, remember?"

Lucas stared at her before nodding.

"Sit down," she ordered, his sudden paleness of concern, and led him to a waiting room chair.

But he sprang to his feet when Dr. Turner appeared. "Doc. How is she?"

At the solemn set of his jaw, dread knotted Willow's stomach. Without shifting her gaze, she reached for Lucas's hand.

"What happened?" Her voice was no more than a whisper.

When Dr. Turner hesitated, her already pounding heart picked up pace.

"I'm so sorry to tell you this...." He paused. Swallowed hard. "But Amelia's had a miscarriage. She's lost the baby."

Lucas shook his head. "She couldn't have. She was fine. She was so happy...."

Willow's vision blurred. The pain of how fast tragedy could strike, how quickly something precious could be taken away, made her chest ache. "Lucas, I'm sorry."

He covered his eyes, crumpled into her arms.

She embraced him once again as she forced herself to be strong.

"Amelia's going to need your support, Lucas." Dr. Turner placed a comforting hand on his shoulder.

Lucas eased away from Willow, swiped a hand over his face. "I understand."

"Take time to grieve, son. Lean on each other during this tragedy, and know we're all here to help you through."

The weight of sadness in the room threatened to overtake Willow as her brother grappled with his and Amelia's loss.

Finally, he exhaled, lifted his chin. "Can I see her?"

Dr. Turner nodded. "She's tired, but she'd want you near."

Willow sniffed as Lucas left her to enter the exam room. Her brother and sister-in-law were two of the strongest people she knew. With God and with each other, they'd make it through. Having someone to depend on in times of sadness made all the difference, making times of trial and heartache bearable.

Jason had once been that strength for her....

WILLOW STARED down at her Styrofoam cup of coffee that had long since grown cold. She set it aside. It was better not to drink it anyway, or it would be difficult to sleep. She pulled a tissue from the box a kind nurse had supplied her with an hour earlier and blew her nose. Caffeinated or not, she'd never be able to rest, not with her grandmother's passing on her heart.

"Darling?" Jason sat beside her on the impersonal, grey hospital waiting room couch. He slipped his arm around her shoulders and drew her to his side. "How are you holding up?"

Willow bit her lip. "Not very well, I'm afraid." She leaned against her fiancé's chest, comforted by the smell of his after-shave and cologne. "I should be glad Grandma isn't suffering anymore. Besides, she was looking forward to meeting her Saviour in heaven and wasn't afraid of death, but it's so painful to think I'll never hear her voice again in this lifetime... or see her smile."

"It's going to be all right," Jason murmured close to her ear. "I'm here for you. I'm not going anywhere."

No words could have reassured her more. She clung to him, knowing even amid this soul-crushing sorrow, the man she loved was by her side. They would make it through together....

. . .

SHE BLINKED, jolting back to the present when Dr. Turner spoke.

"Like I said, Amelia's going to be very tired, but it's best she head home and sleep in her own bed tonight."

Willow nodded. "I'm sure that'll be best." Her mind whirled with the uninvited memory of Jason's support. This was about Lucas and Amelia, but she'd lost the person she'd trusted as her source of support. Instead of being her strength, the man she'd once loved was now her source of pain.

Would the memories ever leave her alone?

Stop tormenting her?

She cleared her throat. "I'll give them some space and head out. I don't want to crowd them, especially when Amelia's exhausted."

Sympathy softened the tired lines of Dr. Turner's face. "I'm sorry, Willow. Take care."

Dangerously close to breaking down once more, she murmured a thank you and took her leave. By the time she reached her car, her lips had twisted. She flattened them to keep the wobble out.

"Why, Lord?" Her hands were stiff on the wheel, her heart as heavy as the grey skies. "Why did You allow this to happen?"

Then her own words came back to her—*Nothing that happens is out of His control.*

If that were the case, why didn't He stop Amelia from miscarrying?

Why didn't He stop Jason from leaving?

When Aunt Charlotte suggested Declan accompany her while she took a meal to Amelia and Lucas, he'd hesitated. As much as he wished to support the couple, he didn't want to intrude on the family during such a difficult time.

Aunt Charlotte had been quick to dismiss his concerns. "They need to know their friends are around them now. Besides, last time I saw him, Lucas told me he misses seeing you at the Youth Centre since he's been spending most of his time at home with Amelia. Seeing you would lift his spirits."

Declan wasn't so sure, but one simply didn't argue with Aunt Charlotte.

At their house, a small whitewashed one once owned by a Greek family, he hopped out of the driver's seat and circled around to the passenger's side to assist his aunt with the ceramic dish of shepherd's pie and pitcher of freshly made lemonade.

Lucas answered the door after she knocked, a warm smile creasing his drawn face. "Charlotte, Declan. It's great to see you both."

She motioned with the food. "I hope you and your bride are hungry because I brought you a feast."

"We'd never turn down a Charlotte-prepared meal. Please, come in. Amelia will be so glad to see you both."

They followed him to the kitchen where they left the food.

"Why don't you both go on in, and I'll dish up a plate for Amelia? Unless, of course, you'd like to join us for dinner?"

Aunt Charlotte waved him off. "I made it for you, but thanks. I'll take her a glass of lemonade. Come on, Declan."

Following his aunt to the couple's bedroom, he paused at their wedding photos displayed on the glossy white hallstand. They both looked so happy and in love with no hints of the challenges ahead of them. Of today, mourning the loss of their unborn baby. But from what he knew of them, they'd support each other while they clung to God, who would sustain and strengthen them.

In the bedroom, his heart jolted. Willow was seated in an armchair by Amelia's bed. Dark circles smudged the delicate skin under her blue eyes, highlighting the unnatural pallor of her tanned face. The past days had taken their toll not only on Amelia but also on her.

"Up for company?" Tiptoeing closer, Aunt Charlotte placed a kiss on Amelia's forehead.

Smiling, Amelia propped herself against the pillows, looking tiny amongst them. "Of course. I'm always happy to see you, Charlotte. And you, Declan."

He gave a nod. Was he supposed to kiss her, too? Probably not. He stood there, hands joined in front of him, aware of Willow's grin. He should've stayed in the kitchen with Lucas. This was women's business, and despite Aunt Charlotte's assurances to the contrary, he was intruding.

She held out the glass to Amelia. "I brought you some lemonade."

"How thoughtful. Thank you." Grasping it with both

hands, Amelia took a long sip, her eyes closing with her sigh. "Lovely as always."

"You're more than welcome, dear. How are you feeling?"

"Better, thank you."

"You don't need to put on a brave face for us. Losing a child, even early in a pregnancy, is never easy."

Wait. Was Aunt Charlotte speaking from experience? She'd lost her husband to cancer when she was young. He hadn't even met Uncle Tom, although he'd seen plenty of his photos in the house. They never had children, and she never remarried. But maybe she'd been pregnant once and miscarried. That would explain her melancholy tone.

His respect for his aunt grew. It was only speculation, but he guessed it to be true.

She continued. "It seems the Lord wanted the blessed child you carried with Him sooner than we expected. But you and Lucas are young. There's plenty of time for God to bless you with other little ones."

But He'd never blessed Aunt Charlotte with little ones. Instead of having children, she lost her husband. And not once had he heard her complain or blame God. Her faith was so strong, and she shared God's love with everyone she met. That was how he came to love the Lord. Not through his parents, but his aunt, his mother's sister. He used to sit and chat with her out on her balcony, ask her how the stars came to be, the sun, the moon, the ocean. His parents never had any satisfying answers but seemed stumped and changed the topic. But Aunt Charlotte told him about God and how He'd created the entire universe from nothing. And how He held it together and made it run like clockwork. And then, one night, she told him about Jesus and the love God had shown when He sent His only Son to earth to be a living sacrifice, the bridge linking Himself and sinful mankind.

Soon after that, Declan decided he wanted to be like Aunt Charlotte, and he accepted Jesus into his life as Lord and Saviour. His parents thought he'd gone crazy. He didn't care. A transformation had occurred inside him, and he knew God was real and this life was just a stepping stone into the next.

And now, imagining more of what Aunt Charlotte may have suffered as a young woman, further convinced him that trusting God was the only way to survive the challenges of this world without growing bitter and twisted. Like someone else he knew... If only his mother would open her heart to the Lord. Instead, her bitterness and resentment were eating her from the inside out.

His gaze swung to Willow. Even with her dark circles, she was gorgeous. A tingle spiralled up his spine. He was falling for her and wanted nothing more than to take her in his arms and comfort her. But he needed to be patient. Healing didn't happen overnight, and he didn't want to lose her by rushing her.

Lucas appeared in the doorway with a small plate of shepherd's pie and made his way to Amelia's side.

Amelia straightened. Looked at the pie and then at Aunt Charlotte. "You made this? It smells amazing. I haven't had much of an appetite, but the smell is making my mouth water."

Aunt Charlotte beamed. "You enjoy, honey. Declan and I will head out now so we don't tire you out. I'll check in with you again tomorrow and bring a pie. I'm headed to the diner now to make a fresh batch of lemon meringue." She grinned at Declan. "I've convinced Declan to come along as my taste-tester."

Amelia chuckled. "Sounds delicious. Willow, you should go with them."

"Yes, come with us, dear." Aunt Charlotte reached out her hand.

But Willow was already shaking her head. "Thanks, but I'll stay here with Amelia."

Amelia's eyes softened. "You've been here every day. You need a break. I'll fall asleep after eating, anyway."

Willow shook her head more adamantly. "I'll stay." She looked from Charlotte to Declan. "But thanks for offering."

Her vulnerability pulled at Declan. He wanted nothing more than to comfort her, assure her he was there for her during this sorrowful time. But he refrained from saying anything other than, "We'll be at the diner for a few hours if you change your mind." Smiling, he tipped his head and made for the door.

"I'll think about it." She pushed to her feet. "I'll see you out."

Oh. Okay.

Aunt Charlotte kissed Amelia, and then followed along.

At the front door, he hesitated while Aunt Charlotte gave Willow a quick hug before making her way to the car.

Willow stood in the doorway with her arms crossed over her chest, and he was so tempted to hug her.

"How are you doing?" he asked instead.

"I'm all right." She rubbed her arms as if chasing away shivers. "I'm trying to be supportive and let Amelia and Lucas know I'm there for them."

"But what about you?"

She frowned, angled her head. "What do you mean?"

He stepped closer and gripped her upper arms. "This tragedy's taking a toll on you. I can see it in your eyes. People are here to support you, too." *Like me.* "As Aunt Charlotte told Amelia, you don't have to put on a brave face."

"I know." Such wistfulness edged that tentative smile.

Keeping his grip on her arms light, he looked deeply into her eyes. "What is it?"

She exhaled. "I've been trying not to make this about me, but I keep thinking about Jason and how supportive he was when my grandmother passed away. Something was reassuring about having someone beside me during that time, someone who'd walk alongside me through the good and the bad. Or, at least, I thought he would...."

"Willow..." His hands tightened on her arms as emotions surged through him. "I want to be careful about how I say this. I wouldn't want to risk scaring you off."

Despite the conversation's sober nature, her eyes glinted. "Scare me off? I'm tough. Go ahead and say it."

At her teasing expression, his chest fluttered. "I'm sure you've noticed I've come to care for you a great deal. I told you there's no pressure to be more than friends, and I stand by that. But I'd love to be the one you turn to for support during this time and any other, happy or sad. I'm here for the long run."

She blinked. "Really?"

More than you know. "Is it such a surprise?"

She ducked her head, her expression going sheepish. "It's just... I've been upfront with you about the turmoil inside of me, and I was afraid you'd run the other way. Your patience and concern astound me."

Heat spread over his skin when she reached up and placed a gentle hand on his cheek. "Thanks for your offer. It means the world to me, and I'll take you up on it."

He cupped his hand over hers. "Wonderful. I'll check in with you soon, okay?"

The peace that settled on her face confirmed he'd done the right thing.

As much as he wanted to convince her to come to the diner, there'd be plenty of time to talk. Right now, she needed to be with her brother and sister-in-law.

Everything else could wait.

After popping *The King and I* into the DVD player, Willow made her way to the kitchen to grab the tray containing two mugs of peppermint tea and a plate of Anzac biscuits from the counter. Back in the living room, Amelia was curled up on the couch, her legs tucked under her, looking well rested from her after-dinner nap.

"Those smell delicious." She smiled as Willow handed her a cup of tea and a biscuit wrapped in a napkin.

"They're compliments of Tish. She came by with the baby while you were asleep."

"Oh. I'm sorry I missed them. I'll have to send a thank-you message. Everyone's been so kind."

Willow settled on the couch with the remote. "They have. It's because they care about you."

They cared about her, too, but everyone seemed more comfortable with a miscarriage than a failed marriage. After Jason left, nobody other than Amelia seemed to know what to do or say, which only made Willow believe she'd done something wrong and caused him to leave. Even her parents had given her strange looks. Of course, they would. Why else would he have taken up with Darlene a month after marrying Willow?

But thanks to Amelia and, more recently, Declan, Willow had left that thinking behind. At last.

"Okay, are you ready for an epic singalong? I haven't seen this movie in years, but I bet I still remember every word to every song."

Amelia regarded her with a sad smile. "It's sweet of you to spend another evening with me."

Willow's brows lowered. "Of course. Why wouldn't I?"

Tenderness softened Amelia's gaze. "I don't know—maybe because you've been here every day since my miscarriage, and you deserve some time to yourself."

Willow waved her off, but Amelia reached over, resting her hand, warm from the mug, on her arm. "I wouldn't have been offended if you'd gone with Declan. It would have been good for you to go."

Snuggling deeper into the cushions, Willow turned her gaze to the TV screen where Mrs. Anna and the king were dancing across the main menu. "I'm happy right here."

"I know you are. But I'm doing okay. I'd like to see you spending time with Declan. He does like you, you know."

Willow's pulse skittered, but she kept her gaze fixed on the screen. If she looked at Amelia, her sister-in-law would see right through her. It had taken every ounce of willpower not to go with him and Charlotte, especially when he said he wanted to be her support person. Support person? Who was he kidding? She could see right through *him*. He was treating her with kid gloves, and she understood why. But the truth was—he *did* like her and wanted them to be more than friends.

And that both excited and scared her.

She flicked some hair over her shoulder. "He's only here to complete the job at the Youth Centre. Once that's finished, he'll be leaving."

Amelia tapped her arm. Lifted a brow. "Charlotte tells me that once he's done here, he hasn't committed to anything else. Maybe he'll find a reason to stay in Water's Edge. Or *someone* to stay for..."

"I don't know what you mean."

A snort sounded. "It doesn't take a genius to see what's going on."

"Oh?" Willow wiggled deeper into her seat. "And what's that, exactly?" How long could she keep up this charade with Amelia? Why was she finding it so hard to be honest?

Amelia's face grew serious. "He's falling for you, and I'd say you're falling for him. Am I wrong?"

Far from it. Declan was the most amazing man she'd met. If only she'd met him before she met Jason. She bobbed her teabag up and down.

But with Amelia's gaze pinned on her, she couldn't avoid responding forever, so Willow finally shook her head. "No, you're not wrong."

"I knew it!"

"Don't get too excited. He's a wonderful man, and he's been nothing but kind, respectful, and considerate."

"But?"

Setting her mug on the side table, Willow wrapped her arms around one of the couch's paisley cushions. "I've come a long way in the past weeks regarding moving on after Jason's betrayal, although it's still hard to understand why God would give me what appeared to be a beautiful gift, only to take it away."

She toyed with the corner of the cushion before lifting her

gaze to Amelia's. "I've wondered that even more when it comes to your miscarriage."

Sighing, Amelia tapped her thumb on the handle of her mug. "It comes down to one fact—God's ways are higher than ours. He sees the big picture. We don't."

The verse played in Willow's head as she let out a low breath. "Isaiah fifty-five."

Amelia's smile wobbled. "I have to believe what He has in mind is so much better than what I've planned. God redeemed my life in such a powerful way when I came to Water's Edge. I was lost, and He swooped me up and placed me ever so gently on the right path. As if that wasn't enough, he then led me to Lucas, a wonderful new family, and reconciliation with my mum before she died." Her eyes shone despite the topic. "He's been so faithful. How can I not trust Him with my current situation?"

Marvelling at her sister-in-law's maturity, Willow chastised herself. Surely if Amelia could trust that God had the circumstances of her miscarriage under control, Willow could leave her own struggles in His capable hands. Yes, He was sovereign, but fully surrendering was easier said than done, although the reward for doing so would be worth the effort.

"You're right. It's funny.... You're so far ahead of me in all this. I do admire you, Amelia. I thank God for the day Charlotte brought you to my little house."

Amelia cuddled back against the cushions, mug cradled in her hand. "It seems so long ago now, although it's not. My life changed when I met you all, and I'll never forget the way everyone embraced me and took me in. I cringe when I think of my old self. I was such a mess."

Tugging at her sister-in-law and sister-in-Christ's sleeve —a blouse Willow had made her—she winked. "I never noticed."

Amelia burst into laughter. "You're a terrible liar."

"Maybe I am. And in more ways than one..."

"Now you're talking."

Willow aimed the remote at the DVD player. "On that note, shall we get this singalong started?"

With an arm around Willow's waist, Amelia hugged her close. "Absolutely."

CHAPTER
ELEVEN

Entering The Coffee Bean Café, Declan glanced around the empty place, then made his way towards the counter. "Hello? Anybody home?" He jolted backwards when Willow popped up from behind the counter, bringing them face-to-face. She jumped as well, her hand flying to her chest.

"Oh my, I wasn't ready for that."

Emboldened by her breathless laugh, Declan rested his elbows on the counter and kept his voice low. "I hope it wasn't too unpleasant."

Her blush said more than words ever could. "Not unpleasant, no. Just unexpected." She cleared her throat and set a bag of coffee beans on the counter. "What can I do for you?"

"I was hoping to bother you for an afternoon pick-me-up. A latte, maybe?"

"Coming right up."

Multiple bags of coffee beans and glass jars lined the counter. "I've heard of people jarring preserves and the like, but coffee beans?"

Her blonde curls swishing, she pulled the espresso shots for his drink. "They're for the Easter Extravaganza."

He picked up one of the jars. "And what do you do with them?"

She finished preparing his drink and set it on the counter before clasping a plastic container. Reaching inside, she unearthed a handful of green coffee beans. "Twenty of these will be mixed with roasted beans and placed in a jar. Whoever separates the unroasted beans from the roasted ones first wins one free drink a week for a month. It's a way to get people interacting with our shop."

He released a low whistle. "One free drink a week, huh? That's pretty generous."

She chuckled at his attempt at humour. "I said that to Sarah, but she said that was all she could manage."

A short silence elapsed as he sipped his drink. It was every bit as good as Charlotte had assured him it would be. However, the luxurious way Willow's beachy curls tumbled over one shoulder distracted him from his latte.

"We all enjoyed the shepherd's pie the other evening, by the way," she said.

"I'll let Charlotte know."

"How was it acting as her lemon meringue pie taste-tester?"

He sent her a thumbs-up. "You know Charlotte. She makes the best meringue around."

"She sure does." Willow hesitated, swirling the green coffee beans around in the container. "It would've been fun to come with you. Maybe you'll consider asking me again sometime?"

Wait. Had he heard correctly? She was giving him a green light? "Ah, yes. You can count on it." Idiot. Why didn't he ask her out, then and there?

She raised her head, and her open expression did strange things to his heart. "I'll hold you to that."

His gaze locked with hers before he cleared his throat. "How–how are Amelia and Lucas?"

"Really well." Willow smiled. "They never cease to amaze me with their trust and strength. After you and Charlotte left, I was talking with Amelia about God's sovereignty. She's so willing to put every circumstance in His hands because of the way He worked things out in her life in the past."

Wise girl. "God does have a way of surprising us, doesn't He?"

"He sure does."

A glint of mischief was the only warning Declan received before a handful of coffee beans flew from Willow's hand, hitting him square in the chest.

His eyes grew wide as he scrambled to catch a few. "What was that for?"

"It surprised you, didn't it?" She teased, sneaking her hand into the bag once again.

"Oh no, you don't." He had his hands on one of the other bags, tossing a handful in her direction before she could blink.

With a squeal, she tossed more beans his way. They continued until they were both breathless with laughter.

"Sorry, I shouldn't be making such a mess in your shop." He leaned on the counter to catch his breath.

"I started it." Flushed, she brushed stray beans from the counter back into one of the bags. "That was a great illustration to prove our point about surprise."

He couldn't have agreed more, but her genuine joy cheered him the most. "Indeed, it was."

She lifted her gaze and met his. It was impossible to look away. With his heart pounding, he leaned towards her, giving her plenty of time to veto his advances. His pulse accelerated when she leaned in as well.

He cupped her cheek, and their lips touched with the utmost tenderness.

Gentle as the gesture had been, he was breathless when they broke apart.

Her face shone.

"I didn't plan for that to happen." His hoarse voice rasped his throat. "But I don't mind telling you I've been wanting to do that for some time."

As she ducked her head and fiddled with her curls, her expression turned shy. "Me, too."

"I hope we can do it again sometime soon." The last thing he wanted to do was push her too quickly.

She beamed, her timidity gone in a flash. "So do I."

If he stayed any longer, no doubt he'd kiss her again. But she was at work, and anyone could come in. Not wanting to embarrass her, he stepped towards the door. "I'd better go. Catch you later?"

Her tanned cheeks had gone a lovely pink. "Yes, you will."

Smiling, he pushed open the door.

"Don't forget your latte." When he glanced back, her brow pointed to his abandoned drink.

With a shake of his head, he returned to the counter and grabbed it.

Her lips were like a magnet, and he could do little but kiss them again before heading out.

It wasn't until he was in his car and driving towards the Youth Centre that he realised he hadn't stayed to help her clean up the coffee beans.

Whoops.

He'd apologise later.

The good thing was that gave him one more reason to see Willow Kelley again as soon as possible.

WILLOW FLOATED on a cloud for the remainder of her shift. The memory of Declan's lips caused goosebumps to rise all over her arms. Amidst everything, how could she be so happy? Amelia was right—she was falling for him and he for her.

She locked up the café, playing the incident over in her

mind. Declan deserved her trust, something she'd thought she would never give again.

After recounting the till three times due to her distracted state, she wrapped up her closing tasks and made her way out to her car. She didn't start the engine. Instead, she stared ahead of her, deep in thought.

That she was considering getting into a new relationship caught her off guard. And yet, an overwhelming peace settled her soul. It felt right. God *had* orchestrated her and Declan's meeting for the right time.

She shivered. Jason had seemed to come at the perfect time as well. Things had been wonderful before everything fell apart...

WILLOW TRIED to still her shaking hands. She'd been trembling nonstop for nearly an hour. She looked at the clock, her chest roiling at how long it was taking Jason to get home. No matter how late he stayed out, he'd have to face her. She had the facts. He'd lied to her. But more than that, he'd been unfaithful.

A growl shot from her throat. "Jason, where are you?"

As if on cue, the front door opened, and her husband's footsteps sounded in the entryway.

Her heart hammered. Her entire body went cold. Until then, she'd felt many emotions—nervousness, anger, fear of loss.

Now she felt only one—crushing sorrow.

Her eyes stung as she looked at the man she loved. When she spoke, her voice cracked. "Jason, h–how could you?"

He pinched the bridge of his nose with two fingers. "Willow..."

Anger flared again, burning away all else. She stepped backwards, shaking her head. "There's nothing you can say. I know you got back together with Darlene only weeks after we were married. A few weeks, Jason." Bitter tears poured down her cheeks. "How could I have been so wrong about you? Why did you pretend with me?"

"It wasn't like that." He stepped towards her.

Her hands flew out in front of her, keeping him safely at arm's length. "Don't! There's no excuse for what you did." The tightness in her throat was strangling her, but she kept on. "No way can you take back the fact that you betrayed me."

His silence confirmed her worst fears. He wanted out. He had no desire to salvage their young marriage. He was finished with her.

Though requesting honesty after his blatant lies seemed futile, she had to try. She'd likely have no other chance. Gathering what little bravery remained, she lifted her chin, stared him straight in the eyes. "Did you ever love me?"

Something flickered over his countenance. Regret?

She held her breath. Would his silence ever end?

"I did love you, yes."

She shook her head, wrapping her arms around herself as the shaking returned. "But not enough to resist being pulled back by one temptation."

He watched her before dropping his gaze to the floor. "I'm sorry, Willow. I didn't mean to hurt you."

Minutes earlier, hearing him say 'I'm sorry' had been one of her greatest desires. Now, as he turned, walking out the door without another word, those two words reminded her he was leaving.

WILLOW JUMPED when her phone buzzed. She pushed away the painful fog of memories when she saw Amelia's name. "Hello?"

"Willow? Thank goodness, you answered. Are you finished at work?"

"I am. What's up? Are you all right?"

"I'm fine. Courtney's gone into labour."

Oh my. Her hand flew to her chest. "But it's too soon."

"I'm worried there's been a complication. She needs to get to the hospital. I'm already here on shift. I called the ambulance, but they're at another job and can't promise to get there outside of an hour. That's too long."

"Don't worry. I'll fetch her."

Amelia's relieved sigh drifted through the phone. "Thank you. Let me know as soon as you arrive."

Willow already had the engine running. "Don't worry about anything. She's going to be all right."

She'd just hung up when Declan's ute pulled into the parking space next to hers. Smiling, he jumped out and headed her way.

"Long time, no see." He grinned when she rolled down the window. "I came back to help with the clean-up. So here I am, in your hair once again."

Had she not been in a rush, Willow might have teased that she didn't mind having him in her hair. No time for that now. "Amelia just called. Courtney's in labour and needs help getting to the hospital. I'm headed to her grandad's now to pick her up. Amelia will meet us there."

Declan was already moving to the passenger side of her car. Now he slid in beside her. "I'll come with you."

Her heart swelled as she drove from the car park. "Thank you."

Her swelling heart fluttered when he reached over and squeezed her shoulder.

"My pleasure. We'll do this together."

By the time they reached Courtney's house, Willow's insides pulsed with growing appreciation for this man beside her.

CHAPTER

TWELVE

eclan pulled the bag of pretzels out of the vending machine, adding it to the two bottles of soft drink and packet of chips he'd already bought. He returned to Willow in the impersonal hospital waiting room. They'd decided to stay until they heard news, even though Amelia had warned it could be hours.

"Thought you might be getting hungry." He held out the selections for Willow's inspection.

"Ooooh, I am. Thank you."

He sat beside her, twisting the lid off one of the bottles as she ripped open the pretzel bag. He watched her, fully recognising the depth of his growing feelings towards her.

A few more moments passed before she looked up from her snack and grinned. "Why are you looking at me like that?"

He tightened his grip on the soda. "Truth?"

Her eyes lit as she angled towards him. "Yes, please."

So he set the soda aside and reached out and took her hand. "I was thinking about our kiss."

Her cheeks flushed. "I've thought about it a lot, too."

He ran his thumb along the back of her hand. "Oh? And what do *you* think about it?"

A coy smile brought out hints of that dimple. "Honestly?"

He nodded, suddenly having no greater desire than to bring that dimple fully to life.

"It was wonderful. But I'm not ready."

Every bit of him deflated.

She took a deep breath and dropped her gaze to their joined hands. "I'm becoming more comfortable about pursuing more than a friendship, but I need to be honest about where I'm at."

This is where she breaks my heart. He steeled himself. "Definitely. I wouldn't want it any other way."

"I'm glad to hear that." She fiddled one-handed with her pretzel before continuing. He could almost see her struggle. "I've been dealing with a lot of memories of Jason lately. The time you came to my house to find me soggy with tears hasn't been my only recent battle." With her heart in her eyes, she looked at him as if letting him in to that heart. "Just when I think I'm open to embracing new experiences and new people, something reminds me of the pain he caused. When that happens, I'm never sure what to do with it. Most often, it makes me wonder if I've made any progress in moving on."

As his heart wrung over her candid admission, he squeezed her hand. "That's understandable. But just because the memories hurt, it doesn't mean you're not healing or moving on. Healing sometimes doesn't result in a complete absence of pain. Knowing what to do with it is the important thing."

She tipped her head, her eyes widening as if understanding had dawned. "I can see that. It's about allowing space to acknowledge and process pain, rather than stuffing it inside and letting it fester."

He drew her hand into his lap, cradling it as he wanted to cradle her. "It's important to hand it to Jesus. I think that's what He meant when He said, 'Come to Me, all you who are weary and burdened, and I will give you rest.'"

"I think you're right." She nibbled the pretzel in her other hand. Stared into the distance. "I've wondered what I'd feel or do if I ever bumped into Jason again. I'm not sure how I'd react."

"If ever it happens, remember you're not alone. Call on God to protect your heart, and remember your worth to Him. Jason can't hurt you unless you allow him to."

She scowled at the pretzel, then lowered it and lifted glowy eyes to him. "I'll try to remember."

He squeezed her hand again as Amelia emerged from the double-swing doors. She strode towards them, beaming.

Willow jumped to her feet. "I gather it's good news?"

"Yes!" Amelia let out a barely contained squeal and clapped her hands. "Courtney's now the mother of a tiny, but perfect, baby girl."

"She was so early, though."

"Well, it seems the dates were wrong. The baby's thirty-six weeks. She's small, but she's breathing on her own. But to be safe, she's in the neonatal unit."

"And what about Courtney?"

"She's in the ward, resting."

"And what about you?"

Amelia's gaze dropped to the floor before she lifted her chin, firmed her lips. "I'm fine."

Willow stepped forward and hugged her.

Declan hovered in the background, feeling like a third wheel until Willow reached for his hand.

Stepping back, Amelia asked if they'd like to see the baby. "You can see her through the glass window."

"We'd love that, wouldn't we?" Willow's inclusion of him warmed him.

"Absolutely."

On their way down the hall, he savoured her tender hand in his. If it was left to him, he'd never let it go. He'd be patient, but with each passing day, he was growing more certain Willow was the woman he wanted by his side for the rest of his life.

If his feelings for her hadn't already been cemented, they would've been by the sheer joy that exploded on her face at the sight of Courtney's baby.

"Oh, Declan, isn't she precious?" She touched her fingers against the glass window separating them from the infants.

"She sure is." Hard as he tried to focus on the baby, he couldn't help enjoying Willow's candid emotions. Unbidden, his mind drifted to what a fantastic mother she'd make. Watching her with the children at church, he'd known she had a heart for them. What would it be like to plan a family with her? Not that he was in any hurry...

When he pulled himself from his daydream, his brow lowered at her solemn expression. He placed a hand on her back. "Everything all right?"

Her gaze remained on the sleeping infant. "I was just thinking."

Wanting to know every detail in her mind, he leaned in closer. "About?"

She hesitated before straightening. "I was thinking about how bleak Courtney's situation was and, in many ways, still is. She doesn't have the stability one needs to care for a newborn, and she's so young, making her future uncertain. And yet God managed to bring something beautiful out of it— this tiny girl, who has her whole life ahead of her."

Wrapping his arm around her shoulders, he smiled at her. "You're right. Even when we don't know how a situation will turn out, we can trust Him, because He does."

With their gazes locked, and unable to resist any longer, he lowered his head and brushed his lips against hers.

THE EVENING FOLLOWING Courtney's long labour, Willow took the Easter decorations to Amelia rather than dragging her out again to work on them at the Youth Centre. Being with

Courtney through her labour had drained Amelia. After her miscarriage, both Lucas and Willow hadn't been keen for her to be involved, but Amelia had insisted.

Now, she needed time to recover.

"Thanks for bringing all this over." She motioned to the assortment of pink, white, and red ribbons and banners strewn over the floor and coffee table. "It must have filled up your entire car."

"It did." Willow laughed as she cut an enormous heart out of construction paper. "But I don't want you to be racing around when you don't need to be. You know what they say: doctors make the worst patients. I think that goes for nurses, too, so someone needs to put their foot down and remind you to take it easy."

Amelia's mouth curved, gratitude glowing in her eyes. "You're always looking out for me. Speaking of looking out for people, thanks for stepping up with Courtney yesterday."

Willow fiddled with the curls of construction paper coming off her heart. "It was the least we could do. Any news on how she's doing?"

"Dr. Turner spoke with the paediatrician this morning. Courtney and the baby are doing well and should be ready to go home in a few days."

The uncertainty awaiting mother and baby once they left the hospital knotted Willow's stomach. "I wonder if Ricky will come around once he meets his great-granddaughter."

Amelia dropped the banner she was adding glitter to into her lap. "He might. Sad as it is, word is that he's washing his hands of them. It's heartbreaking. Courtney's so young and now has her little one's wellbeing on her shoulders. The baby's so sweet. Such an innocent little thing."

"I know." Willow's throat grew thick.

"Of course, Charlotte offered to house them until they can find a permanent situation." Amelia sprinkled more glitter over the banner. "Lucas and I have offered our second bedroom as well since we no longer need it for..." She closed her eyes.

With her heart breaking and unable to imagine the sadness filling her sister-in-law, Willow shuffled closer and rubbed her back.

"Anyhow, there's plenty of help to be had." Sniffing, Amelia straightened her shoulders. "That should buy Courtney time to make some important decisions." She picked up the banner once again. "You and Declan were at the hospital a long time."

"We decided to stay as support for you and Courtney."

Amelia raised a brow. "You must have had a nice chunk of time to talk."

Willow smoothed over an edge of the heart—overdoing it and needing to trim down the other side as well. "I mean, yeah, we talked."

Amelia dropped her project once again and crossed her arms over her chest. "Come on, now. We've established you two are interested in each other. Did you discuss anything about your relationship?"

Willow set the heart aside, sat up straighter, and flung her curls over her shoulder. "Yes, we talked again about how I've been working to move beyond Jason's betrayal." She exhaled, rolling her eyes. "All we do is talk about my past. I don't want Declan thinking I'm talking about it too much."

"It's an integral part of your experience." Amelia lifted a brow. "Does he seem tired of hearing about it?"

Willow's heart warmed as she wrapped her arms around herself. "On the contrary, he's sooo crazy gracious. He's always reminding me the recovery process can't be rushed and is different for everyone. He's so genuine in his understanding."

Amelia rested her chin in her hand. "I can believe that."

"His mother had a traumatic break with his father. His unfaithfulness went on for years before she found out."

"Ouch. That's terrible."

"It is. But it's why he understands what I'm going through. I couldn't have asked for a more sincere listening ear."

Amelia's lips twisted.

Willow leaned forward and gripped her arm. "Did I upset you?"

Waving her off, Amelia set aside her decorating supplies and grabbed a tissue from the box on the coffee table. "I'm just emotional, sorry." She sniffed, managed a smile. "They're happy tears. I'm grateful Declan's been so kind and understanding. After all the heartbreak over losing the baby, hearing things are going well for the two of you and that you're finding healing makes me so happy. God's taking care of both of our hearts, isn't He?"

And how blessed they were. Willow held up a heart featuring a cut out in the middle that fit her face. Looking through it, she smiled at Amelia. "He is."

CHAPTER
THIRTEEN

Declan stood back from the oven, his chest swelling as he surveyed his baked creations. "All right, Aunt Charlotte, want to come and have a taste? I don't mean to brag, but after you try one of these, you're going to want to add Declan's Famous Oatmeal Butterscotch Cookies to your regular menu at the diner."

She puttered into the kitchen doorway, sniffing the air. "You don't have to twist my arm." She came forward, her eyes widening after the first bite. "They're delicious! I didn't realise that, on top of being a talented electrician, you're so skilled in the kitchen."

He ducked his head. "That means a lot coming from the best chef and baker around."

Taking another bite, she scanned the two dozen cookies cooling on the counter. "You made enough to feed an army.

We should share them. Why don't you take a dozen over to Willow?"

"May I ask how it is Willow came to your mind so quickly?"

Shrugging, his aunt became interested in examining the remainder of her cookie. "No particular reason. I thought she might enjoy them."

"Right." He couldn't hide his grin.

With her eyes twinkling, Aunt Charlotte bustled to the fridge. "These cookies are too good not to be accompanied by milk. Grab two glasses from the cupboard, would you?"

He did as instructed, and in no time, they were settled in the living room.

"I love having you around, Deckie," she said, after finishing her second cookie. "But I feel selfish keeping you to myself all the time."

He reached for the pack of cards on the coffee table and removed them from the box. "What are you talking about? I want to be here. The best part of taking this job at the Youth Centre is spending time with my favourite aunt."

"Your *only* aunt." She snorted and snagged another cookie. "Seriously, though, I wouldn't be offended if you wanted to go out tonight."

He sent her a sideways glance as he shuffled the cards. "And who is it you'd like me to go out with, pray tell?"

The sly look slanted her eyes again. "Oh, I don't know." She rubbed the back of her neck. "I do know Willow's off tonight."

"I knew it." He snapped his fingers and pointed the deck of cards at her, stifling his mirth for some semblance of seriousness. "You're great at so many things, but dancing around the point isn't your strong suit. Why don't you just say what's on your mind?"

Sighing, she set her glass on the coffee table before sitting back, the queen of her second domain in her oversized armchair. "I'm not trying to throw you two together, but I'd be lying if I said I didn't think you'd make a great couple."

He shuffled the cards again. "I agree with you."

Her face lit. "You do?"

"I do." He studied the deck, aligning the edges. "I like Willow, and we've broached the subject. We're taking it slowly."

Aunt Charlotte beamed. "So, you've agreed to be more than friends?"

"Not yet." Although, it wouldn't be long.

"You have such a kind and considerate way about you." Her expression thoughtful, she was off the couch and out of the room.

What the...? Jumping to his feet, he followed her into the kitchen. When he entered, she was loading cookies into a Tupperware container. "What are you up to?"

Her determination made him laugh.

"You're taking these to Willow. A little birdie tells me she's been putting in hours at the Youth Centre to help set up for the Easter Extravaganza. Go and rescue her."

He shook his head. "I don't want to rush her."

Aunt Charlotte angled her head like "a little birdie" herself. "I know that girl, and I know she's anxious about loving again. But she needs to know not all men are like Jason Allsopp. Some men exemplify Christ's love in their actions towards the women they care about. You're one of those, Deckie."

Goodness. Heat tingled in his cheeks.

She placed the container in his hands before grasping his arms. "Betrayal can tear a person down, but kindness and respect build a person up and help repair shattered hearts. It takes time, but it's worth the effort. You know that after everything you've been through with your mother."

He studied her, then nodded. "You win. I'll go."

WILLOW PLACED a lid on the box of supplies she'd prepared for one of the many Easter crafts the Youth Centre was planning for the kids. She'd just set it on a shelf with the other crafts when footsteps sounded from behind.

"Every last box is ready, Lucas. I just have to..." Her voice trailed off, her heart skipping a beat when she turned to face, not Lucas, but Declan. She waved a hand. "Oh. I guess you didn't come to ask about the craft boxes."

The lazy smile he sent her warmed her through and through.

"No, but I'd love to hear about them." He settled down into one of the child-sized chairs at a mini table.

She covered her mouth in an attempt to conceal her laughter.

"What?" His eyes held feigned innocence. "Is something funny?"

Unable to control her mirth any longer, she laughed out loud. "Yes, a little."

He scanned the recreation room. "I wanted to see what the kids would experience come Easter. You've done a great job decorating this room. Very colourful and exciting."

"That was the plan." She leaned against the shelf, hugging her arms around herself. "So, what brings you here this evening?"

He held up the container she'd been too distracted to notice. "I'm here on behalf of Charlotte. She insisted I bring you a dozen of the cookies I baked and convince you to take a break."

"Honestly, I haven't eaten since lunch, and a cookie sounds heavenly." She joined him at the kiddie table as he popped off the lid.

He broke off a portion of a soft cookie and held it to her mouth.

She hesitated before accepting it. The brush of his fingers on her lips sent a tingle shooting up her spine.

He leaned in, his attention trained on her as he spoke in a whisper. "Passable?"

She nodded, even though she couldn't taste anything. All she could think about was the man across from her and the intoxicating feel of his breath on her face. With her throat so tight, she wasn't sure she could speak, let alone swallow, but somehow, she managed both. "Why are you here?"

He placed an undemanding kiss on the tip of her nose. "I told Charlotte I didn't want to see you because I didn't want to be too forward."

Her brows lifted as her heart pounded. "Afraid of scaring me off?"

He broke off another bite of cookie and held it up. "Something like that."

Her heart swelling, she reached for his hand. "I don't think you can possibly be any more patient with me. You've given me the space and time I needed while still showing me you care. What I'm trying to say is, you don't need to worry about being too forward."

Edging closer, he rubbed his thumb against her skin. "Then it's not too presumptuous to invite you to dinner?"

The softness in his voice left her tingly. "Not at all."

Leaning forward, he kissed her lips. "Wonderful, but I have a confession."

"You do? And what's that?"

All teasing left his face as his gaze locked with hers. "Charlotte suggested I come and see you, but I've been wanting to ask you out since that day we carpooled to Sydney."

Things had started changing in her that day, too.

But *was* this what the Lord wanted? How would she know for sure?

She looked deeply into his eyes. Clear, honest, and sincere, they peered back, filled with love.

Peace came over her. She could trust this man. She knew it deep down.

How blessed she was to have been given a second chance.

She chuckled when her stomach gave a growl.

Keeping hold of her hand, Declan stood. "Here I am, going on and on, when you haven't had dinner. What would you like?"

"Fish and chips?"

He squeezed her hand, tugging her closer. "Not what I expected you to say. Are you sure you don't want a sit-down meal in a restaurant?"

"Another time? I'm not dressed for anything fancy."

"Fish and chips it is. We can walk along the beach afterwards."

"Sounds perfect."

He didn't waste any time in satisfying her hunger. Within minutes, they were seated at a table in the local fish-and-chip shop, with two pieces of cod and more chips than they could manage.

After eating as much as she could, Willow sat back and wiped her hands on the napkin. "That hit the spot. Thank you."

"My pleasure." Declan drank the last of his Coke before nodding to the sea of games in the adjoining arcade. "Care to play a few games while we're here?"

She rubbed her hands together. "You bet. But beware, I'm rather good and very competitive."

"Let's go. I'm looking forward to seeing your competitive side."

They walked hand-in-hand to the arcade. She stopped in front of the air hockey table. "This one's my favourite. Are you any good?"

He dipped his head, his eyes crinkling up. "I'm all right."

She narrowed her eyes. "I have a feeling you're going to give me a run for my money. You're a terrible liar, you know?"

He leaned over the table, striker in hand, ready to send the puck her way. "Let's allow the game to do the talking, shall we?"

She grabbed her striker. "Game on."

Declan had indeed downplayed his abilities. He beat her the first two games and let her win the third.

"I don't want you to take it easy on me, you know," she said as they made their way to the car-racing games.

He slipped his arm around her waist. "Who said I let you win?"

She gave him a playful shove. "I could tell."

"All right." He waggled a finger in her face. "Next time I won't temper my abilities. You might be sorry, but you've been warned."

When they stepped out of the stuffy arcade an hour later, the night air felt cool and refreshing.

"Too late for that walk?"

While he checked his watch, she scooted ahead and flung out her arms to embrace the night, suddenly feeling like a carefree little girl again. "I won't sleep tonight, so no. Besides, it's a lovely evening."

"It is indeed."

They'd just crossed the road when Harry, a local police officer, came the other way and stopped in front of them. He gave them a nod and folded his arms. "Willow, Declan."

What was going on?

"Ah, how's your evening?" she asked. He might be a member of their church, but he was still a police officer.

"Could be better. I believe you two are familiar with a young lady named Courtney. She's the granddaughter of—"

"Ricky Smith," Willow interjected, her pulse racing. "What's happened? Is she all right?"

His grey moustache flattened as his lips pressed into a thin line. "We don't know. She seems to have disappeared."

She gripped Declan's arm. "How's that possible? She was in the hospital with her baby."

"But she's done a runner."

A lump formed in Willow's throat. "What about the baby?"

Harry shook his head. "Left behind."

As the blood drained from her face, she tightened her grip on Declan, anchoring herself. "What can we do?"

"Any idea where she may have gone?"

When she looked to Declan, he shrugged, so she turned back to Harry. "Amelia knows her best. She might have some idea."

"Tom's already spoken with her. She doesn't know, either."

"I'd like to help with the search," Willow said.

"Me too," Declan added, slipping his arm around her shoulders.

"Any help will be appreciated. This young woman's desperate and scared. Out there on her own, it will only be worse for her."

Wasn't that the truth?

After Harry gave instructions about what areas of town had yet to be scoured, Willow and Declan jumped into his ute and headed to the southern outskirts. Not an area she was familiar with, but one Courtney could have headed to since its cheap housing attracted the unemployed.

Willow prayed silently for her safety as Declan drove slowly, peering down every side street they passed on the way.

CHAPTER
FOURTEEN

Declan scrubbed a hand over his face, working hard to fend off the exhaustion crowding in. They'd been searching for hours and still had no trace of Courtney. He looked over at Willow, who was staring out the window, biting her nails. Reaching over, he placed a hand on her knee. "It's time to give up for the night."

She sighed. "I wish we'd found something to tell us she's okay."

"There's nothing else we can do now. You need to get some sleep."

She crossed her arms over her chest even as her eyelids drooped. "Just a little longer."

He glanced at the handwritten list of areas Harry had asked them to search. "There's one more spot on our way back we can check. After that, I'm taking you to Amelia and Lucas's, no argument."

She blinked at him. "Amelia and Lucas's? Why?"

"Because you shouldn't be alone tonight."

She hesitated, then nodded.

He'd hoped their last destination would provide some sort of clue, but the stop left them as empty-handed as before, offering them no choice but to give up for the night.

Willow's drawn brows and sloping shoulders as he pulled up in front of Lucas and Amelia's house were almost too much to bear.

"Come on," he murmured as he helped her from the car. "You need rest. It's been a long night. I'm sure Courtney will be found."

Willow melted into his chest the moment her feet hit the ground. With little he could do to ease her concerns but provide the comfort of a loving embrace, he happily obliged.

"Thank you for helping with the search tonight," she murmured against his chest.

He drew back, brushing the blonde hair that had escaped her ponytail from her face. "Of course. What's important to you is important to me. I want to be together on this. And in everything. Okay?"

As she gave a grateful nod, he placed an arm around her shoulders. "Come on. Let's get you inside."

His phone buzzed. With great reluctance, he relinquished his hold on her, but his heart raced when Harry's number flashed on the screen.

"Harry?"

"Good news. She's been found."

Exhaling a pent-up breath, Declan nodded to Willow, her eyes enlarging.

"That's fantastic. Thanks for letting us know."

By the time he ended the call, Willow was in front of him, eagerly grasping the front of his shirt. "She's found?"

He rubbed her upper arms. "No need to worry anymore."

The porch lights came on, and Amelia and Lucas stepped outside. "Hey, you guys." Amelia waved them in. "Come inside."

"You go." He looked into Willow's eyes while tucking a strand of hair behind her ear. "I'll head back to Aunt Charlotte's. She'll be a basket case."

Willow smiled as her eyelids began to droop. "Okay. And thank you. See you tomorrow?"

His brow lifted. "Today, you mean?"

"Oh yes. Today."

After leaving her with a kiss to her forehead, he headed home. Sleep would surely elude him, but what did it matter? He'd spend the time praising God, not just for answering his prayers about Courtney but also about Willow.

Like a snuggly warm blanket, peace wrapped around him. God was indeed good.

WILLOW WOKE to the aroma of pancakes and freshly brewed coffee wafting into the bedroom. She blinked. Where was she? The previous evening came back.

Staring at the ceiling in Amelia's spare bedroom, she thanked God that Courtney had been found. Although that was just the beginning of the girl's journey. She'd now be interviewed by the police and the Department of Child Services. She might even lose the baby.

Saddened, she flopped onto her other side. But last night with Declan... Her lips lifted in a smile, and she stretched out on her back. What a fun evening they'd had! And what about that peace she'd felt when she looked into his eyes?

Lord, I'm ready to trust You with all my heart. Thank You for bringing Declan into my life. Guide and lead us as we embark on this new relationship. I only want to do Your will.

She checked her phone, her heart quickening at a text from Declan.

DINNER TONIGHT? I WAS THINKING CHARLOTTE'S MIGHT BE A GOOD COMPROMISE BETWEEN TOO FANCY AND FISH AND CHIPS.

She messaged back that it sounded perfect.

After climbing out of bed, she grabbed the dressing gown from the hook behind the door. Dressed in Amelia's pyjamas and gown, she padded to the kitchen.

Amelia, seated at the table with a plate of pancakes, saluted her with a glass of orange juice. "Good morning, sleepyhead."

Willow sat across from her. "I couldn't get myself up."

"A sleep-in was well-deserved after last night. Pancakes?"

"Yes, please." She eagerly accepted the coffee and pancakes Amelia brought to the table.

"So, how was your evening with Declan?"

Attempting nonchalance, Willow poured a generous amount of syrup over the pancakes. "It was good." When she looked up, Amelia's brow had risen.

Willow chuckled. "All right. It was amazing."

"Great. I'm so happy for you. He's a good man." Amelia opened her mouth as though to pry for details when her phone pinged.

Willow scooped several syrupy bites before lowering her fork. How long *had* Amelia been staring at that message? "Everything okay?"

"I'm not sure." Amelia's brow had puckered. She waved the phone. "It's Dr. Turner. Courtney wants to speak with me about her baby."

Something inside Willow jolted. She pushed her plate aside and reached for Amelia's free hand. "What about?"

"He wasn't specific." She turned her shaky fingers to thread through Willow's. "Would you come with me?"

Of course, she'd go. Willow finished her breakfast quickly, her thoughts on the meeting. What did Courtney want? Moral support for her meeting with DOCS? Naturally, a young woman in her situation would reach out to those who'd been kind to her during this time.

When they arrived at Dr. Turner's office at promptly nine o'clock, he offered an anxious smile. "Thank you both for coming."

"Is everything all right?" Amelia asked.

His lips pressed into a firm line. "I'm not sure. She wouldn't say much. She only wants to speak with you."

Amelia's gaze strayed to the door at the end of the hall. "She's in the consultation room?"

"Yes. I'll be here doing paperwork if you need me. The meeting with the DOCS officer is scheduled for ten."

"Okay." Amelia grabbed Willow's arm. "Come with me?"

Nodding, Willow followed her down the hall to the clinic's consultation room.

Pale and apparently nervous, Courtney wiggled in one of the chairs. Other than that, she appeared to be well physically, which was a relief.

"Hi, Courtney." Amelia greeted in a soothing tone. "How are you?"

The girl stood, folded her arms across her chest. "I'm all right."

"We were all worried about you." Willow stepped forward and squeezed her hand. "We were so happy to learn you were safe. I know you wanted to talk to Amelia alone, so I can leave if you like—"

"No, it's okay." Courtney freed her hand, notching her chin up a bit. "You can hear what I have to say."

Willow's stomach knotted while her sister-in-law remained composed and spoke professionally. "If you're sure, why don't we sit?"

Once settled, Amelia didn't rush Courtney, giving her as much time as she needed.

The girl fiddled with her hands. Her stringy black hair flipped into her face. She obviously hadn't had it trimmed in months. "You both know my grandad didn't support me during my pregnancy?"

"Yes." The gentleness in Amelia's response soothed Willow. She found herself relaxing a bit in her chair.

Courtney exhaled. "Now that Ivy—that's what I decided to name the baby—is here, he's even less supportive." Tears pooled in her eyes. "I can't give her the life she deserves. I don't even know what my future's going to look like."

Amelia laid a hand on her arm. "Many folks here in Water's Edge have already offered aid. They're ready to help in every way—"

"No." Courtney cleared her throat. "I mean, I appreciate that, but I don't want to stay in town. Actually, I *can't*."

Willow and Amelia exchanged glances.

"Where will you go?" Willow asked, remembering what Charlotte had said about her having no other family.

"I don't know. But wherever I go, I can't take Ivy with me."

Sadness cracked Amelia's composure. "Oh, Courtney..."

The girl raised a hand, her expression hardening. "*Do not* try to convince me to change my mind. This is the right thing. I'm putting her up for adoption so she can be raised by a family who can give her a good life." Swiping her hands over her damp cheeks, she released a shaky breath. "It's for the best."

Amelia blinked. Willow could only imagine her turmoil. Amelia would have done *anything* to give birth to a healthy child, making the thought of giving up a baby unbearable.

"You shouldn't make any hasty decisions."

142

Courtney shook her head. "I won't regret it. I've made up my mind."

"You can talk to a counsellor."

"No."

"Okay." Amelia squeezed the girl's hand. "We'll"—her voice cracked, coming out tight with emotion—"do *everything* to ensure Ivy goes to a good home."

Courtney sniffed. "Thank you." Standing, she pulled her worn hoodie tighter around herself. "I'm going now. Thank you for hearing me out, and thank you for all your help."

"You're more than welcome. And don't disappear. You still need care. You've just had a baby."

"I'll be fine." Her wan smile and raised chin left Willow achy.

After she left, Willow could barely lift her head against the heavy sadness in the room. "That's tragic," she whispered.

"Poor Ivy," Amelia murmured, her voice clogged. "She did nothing to deserve this."

"No, she didn't."

Amelia stood to her feet. "Come on. We need to see the doc."

He was alone, his face pinched.

"She told you?" Amelia angled her head.

Nodding, he leaned back in his chair and folded his arms. "She asked if I could make the arrangements with the authorities. I've seen these kinds of situations before, but they never get any easier. But heartbreaking as it is, it might be for the best. That girl would struggle to raise her baby, even if she loved her."

Amelia shifted her weight, her gaze on the ground. "We'll adopt the baby."

Willow's eyelids shot open. "You'll—what?"

Amelia's gaze lifted, confidence firming her expression. "Lucas and I will take little Ivy."

Her words dropped like stones into the sudden silence.

Then Dr. Turner spoke. "Don't make a rushed decision. You've been through so much, Amelia."

She lifted her chin. "But don't you see that's why this makes sense? Lucas and I lost our little one, and now Ivy's lost her mother. We're all in need of comfort and God's provision right now, and this is our chance to take hold of that. Maybe this was His plan all along—to make Lucas and me available to Ivy. And Ivy available to us."

It did make sense, but gracious, it was a huge thing. Adopt Ivy? Wow. "What about Lucas?" Willow said. "Shouldn't he have a say?"

"Of course. But he'll be in agreement, I know it." Amelia turned to Dr. Turner. "Will you hold off on arranging anything until I get back to you? Running it past Lucas is only a formality—I already know what he'll say."

"Sure. I'll wait until I've heard from you. I guess congratulations are in order."

"Thank you. This feels so right."

And it did. After the initial shock, assurance this was indeed of God settled in Willow's heart.

What no eye has seen, what no ear has heard, and what no human mind has conceived—the things God has prepared for those who love Him.

His provision was amazing. And not just for Amelia, Lucas, and Ivy but also for her.

CHAPTER
FIFTEEN

When Amelia rushed inside Lucas's office, eyes large, round, and shiny, his heart lurched as his fingers stilled over his keyboard. Something was up. "Hey, hon. I didn't expect to see you this morning."

"No. But we need to talk."

"Okay..." Closing his laptop, he gave her his full attention.

She perched on the edge of his wooden desk, arms crossed, and leaned forward. "God's answered our prayers."

"I know He did. Courtney was found."

"Yes, but He's also given us a baby."

His heart lurched again, and his mouth gaped. "What do you mean?"

"She's giving the baby up for adoption." She leaned forward. Clasped his hand. "Let's take her, Lucas. It feels so right. We lost our little one, and now Courtney's baby needs a mother and a father. I want to do it."

Her eyes were even larger. His mind swirled. "Can we pray about it?"

"Sure. But I'm convinced already."

He studied her. Was it such a harebrained idea? Although their pregnancy had been unplanned, they'd both warmed to the idea of being parents, and the miscarriage devastated them.

They'd not considered adoption, but perhaps this was of God. He waved her over, pulled her onto his lap, and traced a finger around her hairline. "Tell me what happened."

"Courtney asked to speak with me. When I met with her, she told me she was giving Ivy, that's what she's called the baby, up for adoption. She couldn't give her the care she deserved."

"How do you know she won't change her mind?"

"She was adamant, and I believed her. She's not in a good way, and I respect her for making such a difficult decision."

Moments passed. Although he'd never turn anyone in need away, this was a huge decision.

"Maybe we could start by fostering and see how it goes. Adoption will take time as there's a lot of red tape to go through."

"So, that's a yes?" Her whole body stiffened. Was she holding her breath?

He inhaled the slow breath he wanted her to take. "Let's pray about it?"

She was wanting an answer, but he needed an answer from God first. No doubt she had prayed already, but he, too, needed peace. Taking on a child was a lifetime commitment.

He placed his hand over hers and bowed his head. "Lord, our hearts go out to Courtney. I can't even imagine how she feels. Wrap Your arms around her, protect her, draw her to Yourself. And please give us guidance regarding the baby. Don't let us make a rash decision we might regret, but if it is of You and You wish us to be her parents, give us peace and assure us this is the path You wish us to take. Thank You for Amelia and her willingness to love those who need it the most. Thank You for her kind heart. I pray all these things in Jesus' precious name. Amen."

"Amen." Amelia raised her head. Looked at him expectantly.

Something inside him tingled, and as the words from Mark 9 came to him, he took it as double confirmation. *Whoever welcomes one of these little children in My name welcomes Me; and whoever welcomes Me does not welcome Me but the one who sent Me.*

He smiled at her. "Okay. Let's do it."

Beaming, she threw her arms around his neck, but short shaky breaths shuddered through her.

"Hon." He rubbed her back and held her close, his own heart bursting. God *had* turned their ashes into joy and replaced their mourning with a garment of praise. How great was their God?

When her sobbing eased, she straightened and brushed

her cheeks. "I'll call Doc and find out what we need to do. And then, let's go to the hospital and see our baby."

Their baby. And they didn't need to wait nine months. She was already here.

CHAPTER
SIXTEEN

That night, seated in a booth in Charlotte's diner opposite Willow, Declan shook his head. "Crazy that Lucas and Amelia are adopting Ivy. Don't get me wrong, it's great, but unexpected."

Willow stirred her chocolate thickshake with a long striped straw. "I know what you mean. It took me by surprise, too, but I've never seen them so happy."

Their burgers arrived, but although they looked and smelled delicious, Declan didn't immediately dig in. "We should give thanks."

Willow nodded. "Good idea."

Reaching for her hand, he bowed his head. Since so many things had happened, it was hard to know where to start. Inhaling deeply, he centred his focus on the Lord. "Heavenly Father, thank You for Your amazing love, which is beyond measure and undeserved. Thank You for Your many blessings, which are also above and beyond. Bless Amelia, Lucas, and Ivy as they embark on this new chapter in their lives. It's such a huge thing, but I know You'll go before them and prepare each step. And bless Courtney, Lord. She must be feeling heartbroken and lost. May she turn to You for comfort and guidance. Please protect her. And thank You for bringing Willow into my life. I feel so blessed to know her. Help me love and respect her the way You would want me to. And lastly, thank You for this food. Bless it to our bodies. In Jesus' precious name. Amen."

"Amen," Willow repeated, a sheen covering her eyes when she opened them.

He squeezed her hand. With soft curls tumbling over her shoulder and her smile as warm as a spring day, he never wanted to let go of her. But he couldn't hold off any longer. His burger awaited. He'd gone for the Water's Edge Classic, while she'd chosen the Crispy Chicken Supreme. A generous serving of fries filled the basket in the middle of the table.

He bit into his burger and thought he'd gone to heaven as robust flavours burst in his mouth. Aunt Charlotte sure knew her stuff.

Willow chewed thoughtfully. "Charlotte and Mum have offered to watch Ivy while Amelia's in school. I have a feeling they're going to end up fighting over who gets to look after her most."

Declan chuckled. When Aunt Charlotte gave him the news, she could hardly stand still, seeming even more excited about getting to babysit than about the adoption itself. Maybe this was God's way of blessing her with a little one since she'd never have grandchildren of her own.

As he dug into his burger, Willow set hers down.

"Something wrong?" He wiped his mouth with a napkin.

She shook her head. "I was just thinking that God *does* work all things for good for those who love Him. It might not happen immediately, but if we're trusting Him, we can be sure He has our back, even if we mess things up along the way. He can turn even the bleakest situation around. Amelia and Lucas were devastated when they lost their baby, but look at them now. They couldn't be happier. And then there's me. It took me time to process what happened with Jason. I still feel embarrassed about it, but when I thought I might never find happiness again, He brought you into my life. Because of you, I have hope I can love again."

Setting his burger down, he reached across the table and traced a finger along the back of her delicate hand. "And because of you, I have hope, one day, my mum will turn a corner."

She pressed her other hand to her chest. "That's such a lovely thing to say. And I'm sure she will. Sometimes it just takes a while."

She had that right. "In the meantime, God's teaching me patience."

"You're doing great with her. She's blessed that you care so much."

Their gazes locked. "Would–would you like to meet her?" He hadn't planned to ask, but somehow, it seemed right.

Moments passed, and the diner sounds receded while the fries' smell clogged his nose. Had he asked too much?

Then she nodded. "I'd love to."

He flopped against the seat. "Great. We'll have to figure out the best time to go."

"Things will be crazy around here for the next week or so."

"Oh, yeah." He leaned forward again. "That brings me to the next question."

"And what might that be?" She angled her head, her eyes twinkling.

"Would you like to be my date for the bush dance?"

Lips twitching upward, dimple winking, she flicked some hair off her shoulder. "I was wondering if you'd ever ask!"

Joy bubbled inside him. "I take it that's a yes?"

"It's a yes and yes."

"Wonderful! Now, I need some dancing lessons between now and tomorrow night."

She laughed, the motion sending her curls dancing on her shoulders. "There's a caller. You just follow what he says."

"Oh. Right." He clicked his fingers. "Of course. It's a bush dance."

"Yep. Get your cowboy boots on."

"Yeehaw!"

Curls still shaking, she picked up her burger and dug in.

CHAPTER
SEVENTEEN

The following morning, Declan headed to the sports field to help set up for the bush dance. He thought he was early enough, but by the time he arrived, activities were already in full swing. With the marquee being erected and plenty there to help, he stepped in and supported one of the poles until they'd secured it with a rope and peg. Although the breeze was light, it never paid to take a chance, especially in a coastal town.

He found Lucas and was charged with overseeing all the electrical requirements. A three-piece band would be playing, and the sound system would be critical for not only the music but also the caller. Lighting also needed to be installed. He had a team of three to work with, and all the equipment had been hired and was ready and waiting. He rubbed his hands together. "Right, let's get this show on the road."

Four hours later, everyone broke for lunch. The actual

event might not have formally commenced, but like a well-oiled machine, trestle tables appeared, barbecues were fired up, and tubs of food laid out.

When Willow approached, her ponytail swinging from side to side, her face beaming, he grinned. "I didn't know you were coming."

"I thought I'd bring you a treat."

"Just seeing you is treat enough."

She burst into laughter. "You're too funny."

"I'm deadly serious."

"Well, anyway. I brought some fudge. And some watermelon."

"Sounds great. Are you staying for lunch?"

"No, I need to get back. I just had a short break, but I'll see you tonight."

"You sure will. Pick you up at six?"

"I'll be raring to go." She flashed a smile that reached under his skin, all the way to his heart.

WILLOW HURRIED home from work and showered. Being so eager to attend the bush dance still amazed her. Also, being able to think about it without any heartache. Who'd believe she'd ever move past the pain? She wouldn't have a year ago, but God had given her a hope and a future. It was early days with Declan, but surely, this time, God had brought the man of her dreams into her life. He'd used her experience with

Jason to grow her, to mature her, and to teach her what it meant to trust Him, and she couldn't wait to see what the future held.

She dressed in her best blue jeans, a red-checked button-up shirt with sleeves rolled to the elbows, and knee-high boots. She topped the outfit with an Akubra hat.

After applying a light coat of makeup, she stepped back from the mirror and smiled when Declan's ute pulled up.

Nudging the curtain aside, she glanced out the window, and her heart fluttered. He carried a huge bunch of flowers and looked so, so handsome. Dropping the curtain, she pressed a hand to her chest to calm her pounding heart.

To no avail. When he knocked on the door and she opened it, her heart beat even faster, and his smile hit her blood like an espresso shot. He handed her the flowers and framed her face with his hands. His lips brushed hers, and he kissed her slowly and gently, leaving her breathless.

They drove to the dance in his ute, her hand on his thigh. With the band already warming up, she couldn't wait to get her feet moving.

Before the dancing began, the band took a break, and Lucas walked onto the stage. He tapped the microphone to get the attention of everyone there, several hundred people. Men, women, children, grandparents, aunties, and uncles.

"Hello, everyone. Welcome to this year's Easter Extravaganza. We're thrilled to have you all here, and we're excited for the events of the entire week, kicking off with tonight's dance. But first, let's pause to give thanks to our Lord. Easter is when we remember the sacrifice Jesus made so we can have peace with God. He gave His life on our behalf, but He didn't stay dead. He rose and lives today, giving assurance of eternal life to those who believe. Will you pray with me?"

He paused, and everyone bowed their heads.

"Lord God, we thank You for Your sacrificial love and the assurance we have that this life is not all there is. However, we also give thanks that we can enjoy life in the here and now, and we ask Your blessing on the events we've planned for the week, including this bush dance. Help us to enjoy each other's company and look out for each other. We thank You for this tightly knit community, but we know folks out there are hurting and lonely. Give us caring hearts that we might put others' wellbeing before our own. We ask all these things in the name of our Lord and Saviour. Amen."

Amens resounded throughout the marquee. The band members returned to the stage. The caller, a man in his sixties who'd been calling bush dances for years, stepped up to the microphone. "Right y'all. Take your partners for an old-fashioned barn dance."

The music began, and Declan slipped his arm around her waist and whisked her to the circle forming.

"I didn't think you knew how to dance."

He winked at her. "I was having you on."

She chuckled and leaned into him. She was going to have a great night!

And she did. By the time midnight came, she was exhausted but happy. He dropped her at home and promised to see her again the following day. She was manning the coffee stand, but Sarah had given her the afternoon off.

And so, the week passed. When Good Friday came, she paused by her bed, dropping to her knees to thank Jesus for His ultimate sacrifice and to centre her heart on Him before the service. With the euphoria of new love heightening her senses, it wasn't hard to pour out her heart in gratitude.

Declan drove her to church, and they sat alongside Mum, Dad, Amelia, Lucas, baby Ivy, and Charlotte. Mum and Charlotte hovered over baby Ivy, who had been discharged from the hospital into Amelia and Lucas's care. Formal adoption was still a way off, but nobody anticipated any issues.

Willow's heart warmed at the love everyone had for Ivy. She was such a tiny thing, only five and a half pounds. But she had strong lungs, and she loved her milk. And, she was very much wanted. She would grow up in a stable, loving family. Exactly what Courtney had wanted for her.

The service began with the hymn 'When I Survey the Wondrous Cross'. Willow couldn't think of a better song to start with. She stood with Declan and held his hand.

> When I survey the wondrous cross
> On which the Prince of Glory died,
> My richest gain I count but loss,
> And pour contempt on all my pride.
> Forbid it, Lord, that I should boast,
> Save in the death of Christ my Lord!
> All the vain things that charm me most,

I sacrifice them to His blood.

See from His head, His hands, His feet,

Sorrow and love flow mingled down!

Did e'er such love and sorrow meet,

Or thorns compose so rich a crown?

Were the whole realm of nature mine,

That were an offering far too small;

Love so amazing, so divine,

Demands my soul, my life, my all.

THE WORSHIP LEADER bowed his head. "Lord, we come before You this Good Friday in humble adoration as we survey the empty cross. Love so amazing, so divine, demands our soul, our lives, our all. We thank You for Your amazing gift, and we humbly ask for Your blessing today. May the eyes of any who don't know You yet be opened to this amazing love. In Jesus' precious name. Amen."

The youth performed a dance item depicting the anguish the disciples felt when Jesus hung on the cross. Although He'd told them what was to happen, they didn't understand. It wasn't until after He rose on the third day that hope was restored. And what about the year of darkness she'd been through? God had promised He wouldn't leave her in the valley, and He'd kept His promise.

Pastor Noah's sermon was just as touching, and at the end

of the service, ten people gave their hearts to the Lord for the first time.

Afterwards, their family and Charlotte, who was considered family even before Willow had taken up with Declan, gathered at Mum and Dad's for lunch, giving plenty of time for cuddles with baby Ivy.

Later, once lunch was finished and Amelia and Lucas said they'd like to take Ivy home, Willow asked Declan if now was a good time to visit his mother.

His eyes had widened, but then he said, "Sure. Why not? She'll be at home."

Cupping his cheek, Willow leaned up and planted a kiss on his lips. "Okay. Let's go."

EIGHTEEN

Declan glanced at Willow sitting beside him on their impromptu trip to Sydney. He was learning to love that about her. Aunt Charlotte had told him she'd been vivacious and spontaneous before Jason, but his betrayal had stolen her zeal. But now it was back. She'd outdanced him at the bush dance, outsung him in church, and surprised him with this outing.

Mum, too, had been taken aback. "You won't get here until late afternoon."

"Does it matter? We'll bring dinner."

"Did you say *we'll* bring dinner?"

"I did, Mum. I'm bringing a girl to meet you."

"Well, I never. I hope she doesn't mind a dirty house."

"It won't worry her in the slightest."

Mum grunted. "Okay, then. But I don't know why you're bothering bringing her to see me."

"She wants to meet you."

"I don't know why. She'll change her mind when she gets here."

Mum would say that. He'd nearly ground his teeth. "Let her decide that, hey? We'll be there in about two hours."

"Whatever."

Declan had groaned as he ended the call. At least she'd sounded sober.

Now, they were mere moments away. He reached out and squeezed Willow's hand. "Are you sure you're up for this?"

She clasped his hand back. "More than up for it. I'm looking forward to it—don't forget how well I already know her."

What *had* he done to deserve this woman? He slowed to take the final corner.

The grass was no longer brown, thanks to recent rain, but the lawn was overgrown. As he pulled into the driveway, he faced her. "Mum said the house is dirty, too. I apologise in advance."

"I'm not here to cast judgement. It's fine, really. Don't worry. Please."

He inhaled deeply. Prayed silently. *Lord, please let this go well.*

Willow opened her door. Climbed out. Stretched. "So, this is where you grew up."

"Yep."

"It's close to the uni."

"It is. That's why they moved here. It suited Dad."

Her gaze roamed the short cul-de-sac filled with double-story brick homes. Mature trees provided shade, and all the gardens were well tended. All apart from one. He needed to spend time up here. Or pay for a gardener.

She removed her sunglasses as the sun dipped below the tree line. "It's not so bad."

He held his hands up. "It's not Water's Edge."

Her eyes sparkled. "Good point."

He walked around and took her hand. "I appreciate you doing this."

The slightest hint of her dimple peeped at him as she tucked hair behind her ear. "I *want* to meet your mum."

His heart swelled. She was a keeper, for sure.

They walked to the door, and he almost fell over backwards. Mum stood in the doorway, dressed in dark slacks and a beige knit top. She'd pulled her grey hair back in a tidy bun and added a touch of makeup. Willow probably wouldn't believe what he'd told her about his mum now. But whatever. This was good. She'd made an effort.

"Mum. Nice to see you. Happy Easter." He opened the door and kissed her on the cheek. "This is Willow. Willow, this is my mum, Barbara."

Willow stepped forward and extended her hand. "Nice to meet you, Barbara."

Mum shook Willow's hand and offered a small smile. "And nice to meet you, too. Come in. Please excuse the mess. Declan didn't give me much notice."

"That was my fault. I suggested we come and see you. We

were having lunch with my family, and I felt bad you were alone."

"Oh. That was thoughtful of you. I'm used to it, though."

"I understand."

Her eyes narrowing, Mum stopped and studied Willow. "I'm sorry to be rude, but how would you understand what it's like to be alone?"

Willow shrugged, glanced at Declan, and then faced his mother. "Where do I start?"

Mum's brow scrunched.

He cleared his throat. "How about I make some refreshments while you two get acquainted?" He ushered them into the living room. "Tea?"

Mum nodded. "Yes. No sugar. I'm trying to cut back."

Another good sign. He kissed the top of her head. "I won't be long."

As he headed to the kitchen, he wished he could be a fly on the wall, but unable to achieve that, he *could* pray as he made a pot of tea. He and Willow had brought a batch of Aunt Charlotte's freshly baked hot cross buns. He took three from the container and warmed them in the microwave while the tea steeped.

Then he carried the tray into the living room and set the tea and buns on the coffee table. The room wasn't as bad as he'd expected. Mum must have done a quick tidy up. The kitchen hadn't been that dirty, either.

Quirking an eyebrow, Willow met his gaze as he poured her tea. If only he knew what that meant. One day, he guessed he would, but right now, he was still learning about her. But Mum would notice if he didn't say something. He didn't want her to know he'd invited Willow to talk with her. That could be the end of it. "So, how's your week been, Mum?"

"The same as always."

Hmph. What did that mean? "You've been to work, then?"

"Mostly."

He set her tea on the side table beside the beige uphol-stered chair. "I hope it's how you like it."

She inspected it. "It'll be fine."

That was a first. "Great. I'll sit over here. You two keep talking." He retreated to a recliner in the corner. Dad's recliner. Why hadn't she gotten rid of anything that reminded her of him? Why hadn't she moved? Willow would under-stand that better than he would. He tried not to listen as he flicked through one of Dad's old Physics magazines tucked in the side pocket, but it was almost impossible not to eavesdrop.

"So, what helped you to move on?" Mum asked.

Willow took a moment to answer. "A combination of many things. I was growing tired of being down all the time, but getting motivated to do anything to change that was hard. Declan helped me a lot. He listened. He told me things that made sense, like that my worth wasn't tied up with Jason's betrayal. I stopped blaming myself, and I stopped blaming God. I forced myself to do something different, so I took up jogging."

Declan grinned, thinking of the day they bumped into each other on the beach.

"But the main turning point came when I started being honest and not trying to pretend I was okay."

Mum stirred her tea, her eyes crinkling up before she winked. "Declan will tell you I gave up pretending years ago."

"Everyone's journey is different." Willow set aside her own tea to test a hot cross bun. "I can't tell you what to do, but you'll turn a corner if you can start doing one thing different. And then, later, something else."

"I've cut back on sugar."

"That's a great start. You should celebrate that. It doesn't seem like much, but when you're at rock bottom, any baby step is huge. And you go to work. That's applaudable. You're doing great."

Mum's eyes glistened. "That's kind of you to say so. I don't think I am, but maybe there's light at the end of the tunnel."

"There is. And you never know what's in store for you." Willow faced Declan, her eyes aglow. "Look what happened to me."

"I doubt anyone would give me a second glance."

"You never know. It's never too late to fall in love again."

"Well, young lady, you've given me much to think about. If I'm honest, I'm fed up with my life."

"Why don't you move? You could come and live in Water's Edge. It's a great place, isn't it, Declan?"

He gave a nod. Sure was. All *he* had to do was figure out how to stay there now his work was about finished.

Mum's forehead creased. "I *could* visit my sister."

"Yes! Charlotte would love to have you visit, wouldn't she, Declan?"

He nodded again and gripped his knees to keep from springing out of his chair. Was this happening? Mum was considering visiting Aunt Charlotte?

"Come back with us tonight." Willow touched Mum's forearm. "It's a long weekend, after all."

Declan held his breath. She'd gone too far. Mum would retreat. She didn't like being pushed.

"Let me think about it."

His eyelids shot open, and his fingernails dug into his kneecaps. She was thinking about it? Good grief. Why hadn't he brought Willow sooner?

"That's great." Willow sank back into her chair and broke off a bite from Aunt Charlotte's bun. "There's no pressure, but you'd be welcome if you decided to come."

Mum returned her smile with a small one of her own, then faced him. "You said you were bringing dinner."

He straightened, put the footrest down with a clunk. "We did. I grabbed one of Aunt Charlotte's meals from her freezer. She always has a good stock. Would you like me to get it ready now?" It was only five, and Mum had only nibbled her bun. But whatever.

She glanced at the clock. "I'm thinking we shouldn't leave it too late to be on the road."

His mouth gaped. She was coming? "Okay. I'll get it ready now. And I'll call Aunt Charlotte and let her know to make up another bed."

"So long as you're sure she won't mind."

"She won't mind at all—she'll be so excited to see you that I can picture her happy dancing or making up some special treat for when you arrive. Maybe you could pack a bag while I get dinner ready?"

"I don't believe I'm doing this, but it's because of you, Willow. You gave me hope. Thank you." Her eyes glistened again and, this time, overflowed.

Willow stood and went to her. Hugged her. Held her. "You're more than welcome. I'm glad I could help."

She smiled at him over the top of his mother's head.

Joy welled inside him as he sent up a grateful prayer.

They had dinner and then drove back to Water's Edge in the dark. Willow squeezed into the back seat intended for small children so Mum could sit in the front. He had to keep looking at her to make sure he wasn't dreaming.

Aunt Charlotte welcomed her with open arms and a broad smile. "It's so good to see you, Barbara. You're looking well." She winked at Declan as she slipped her arm around Mum's shoulders.

They walked inside together while he stayed outside with Willow. Leaning against his ute, he pulled her to him, palmed her cheek. Gazed into her eyes. "I don't know how you did it, but you worked a miracle today."

"Not me. I just told my story. That's all. God did the rest."

"Well, you're a good team."

Her curls tickled his hands with her quick headshake.

"You did the groundwork, don't forget. It's easy to see the outcome and forget all that went before it. Without you to support her over the years, she might have sunk even further."

He wasn't sure how that could be, but Willow might be right. It didn't matter. All that mattered was that Mum had turned a corner. A major one, although another major one remained. Full surrender to God. He'd keep praying.

"Thank you." He kept her face framed between his hands, holding her in place as he let himself sink deep into her eyes, breathe deeply of her scent. "You know, you have such a gift. I know your heart's set on having your boutique, but maybe you should consider a dual career."

Her head tipped sideways as she eyed him. "What's that?"

"Fashion and counselling. You told me that, before Jason, you were the one who offered advice to people."

"Hmm. I'm not so sure, but I'll give it some thought. I still have a lot to learn." She lifted her hand and placed it over his.

"Don't we all?"

She nodded. "I guess so."

His gaze was drawn to her lips, parted and full, and the sound of her shallow breathing filled him with longing. In slow motion, he bent towards her, closing his eyes to caress her mouth with his own. Drawing her close, he cupped the back of her neck and kissed her deeply, his fingers twining in her hair.

Then he forced himself to end the kiss. "I'm sorry. I got carried away."

"Don't be. You're the best thing that's ever happened to me."

Smiling, he struggled with the emotions swirling inside him. "And you're the best thing that's happened to me, but I don't want to ruin it. I want us to get to know each other and not rush anything. I'll tell you now that I want to spend the rest of my life with you, but there's no hurry. Let's take it slowly, commit our relationship to the Lord, and take a step at a time."

"I respect you for that. It'd be too easy to rush, and I want this to last. We do have plenty of time."

He took her hand and pressed a kiss to her palm. "I love you, Willow. We haven't known each other long, but it feels like I've always known you. Be assured I'll always do the right thing by you."

A sheen covered her eyes. "I love you, too, Declan, and I promise the same. I'll always do the right thing by you."

His chest warmed as he grinned. "Now that's settled, we should go inside, or Mum and Aunt Charlotte will wonder what we've been up to."

Giving a slight eye roll, she nudged him with an elbow. "It wouldn't surprise me if your aunt hasn't been peeking out the window."

He winked back. "You might be right."

CHAPTER
NINETEEN

Had Willow not been on a time frame, she might have bought every item in the baby store. After finishing her classes, she'd intended to stop by the baby shop to buy only a few things for baby Ivy, but Willow ended up walking out with multiple onesies and sleepers, an adorable cardigan with teddy bear ears, tiny, pink tennis shoes, and miniature socks. She spent a small fortune, but she had no regrets as she loaded her purchases into the car.

Everyone was aglow over welcoming Ivy into the Kelley family. The adoption process, spanning only a couple of weeks, had been completed in record-breaking time as all parties were in agreement about what was best for Ivy. Though this simplified things, God's hand over it all was the real reason for the smooth process.

After consulting the clock, she opted to stop at Dr. Turner's office. Amelia would be there with Ivy, who was scheduled for her baby-wellness exam. Willow couldn't wait to show her sister-in-law the baby clothes, but getting to visit with baby Ivy was a chance she couldn't pass up.

As she parked in the car park and gathered her bags, nothing but the wonder of it all filled her mind. She was so distracted that, upon entering the front office, she simply dropped her shopping bags into a pile next to Dr. Turner's desk and was about to call out to see where everyone was, when she froze. She wasn't alone.

A man in need of medical attention sat in one of the waiting room chairs. However, the bloodied rag he held around his hand didn't cause her hands to grow cold.

His identity did.

Jason?

He shot to his feet, his face registering the shock she felt.

"W–what are you doing here?" Willow croaked. She cleared her throat. "Are you all right?"

His mouth opened and closed as he glanced at his injury. "I was in the area doing a tyre delivery and cut my hand while unloading the truck. I couldn't drive back to the city without getting it tended to, so I had to come in. I didn't think..."

"That you would see me. You could have gone to the hospital."

"I did. But the wait was too long."

She'd convinced herself she'd never see Jason again, either by accident or design. That chapter of her life was closed, and with the peace she felt in her relationship with Declan, she'd been more than ready to let Jason go for good.

She'd seen no reason to prepare for confrontation, but Declan's words came back to her now—*"Jason can't hurt you unless you allow him to."*

She wouldn't allow him to. God was with her, giving her strength.

He looked much the same as he had a year earlier. His eyes were unchanged. They appeared genuine and sincere to anyone who didn't know him. Had she been the only one who'd seen the betrayal beneath the surface? His blond hair was longer. Darlene's preference? It had been short when he was with Willow.

A muscle in his jaw twitched as he shifted from foot to foot. Willow would've found that glimpse of uncertainty satisfying until recently. Now, she felt little.

Footsteps sounded from the back with Dr. Turner's approach. His eyes widened as he glanced between Jason and her.

"Willow. I didn't know you were stopping by."

"It was a spur-of-the-moment decision. I thought I'd catch Amelia and the baby."

As if on cue, Amelia emerged from the back with Ivy, her mouth gaping.

"I'd just gone to clean the exam room so I could tend to Jason's injury. Little Ivy's appointment is done," Dr. Turner explained.

In the uncomfortable silence, Amelia stepped closer to Willow. Squeezed her hand. "Come for a coffee?"

Willow's gaze narrowed at the man who'd once been her husband. "That would be great. Thanks."

Pulling Ivy's blanket around her tiny frame, Amelia nodded to Jason and ushered Willow outside.

Willow glanced back. "On second thought, let's take a raincheck. I have unfinished business."

Amelia gave a slow nod, understanding passing between them. "Are you sure?"

Willow inhaled. Exhaled. "I need to do this."

"Okay." Amelia hugged her. "I'll be praying for you."

"Thank you."

Back in the empty waiting room, Willow dropped into one of the chairs. Could God have intended this to be an opportunity and not a nightmare she should run from? There had to be a reason for Him allowing their paths to cross again.

As time ticked by, calm settled over her. She wasn't alone.

When the men emerged from the exam room, she'd been praying nonstop for many minutes.

Dr. Turner's forehead creased. "I thought you'd left, Willow."

"I decided to stay." She sent him a smile to assure him she was fine, but his concern remained.

Not surprising. To anyone who knew her, the idea of her sticking around when Jason was in the next room would be unthinkable.

But she needed to speak with him.

She gestured to his bandaged hand. "How is it?"

He opened his mouth, closed it, opened it again. Still tongue-tied?

Dr. Turner stepped in. "A lot of stitches were needed, but it should heal well." He wrote out a script for pain medication and handed it to Jason. "Get those stitches out in two weeks. Do you have someone to drive you home?"

Jason opened his mouth again. His Adam's apple bobbed as he swallowed. "One of my guys is giving me a lift."

"Good." Dr. Turner opened the front door. "Speedy recovery, Jason."

Though Dr. Turner must have decided ushering Jason from her would be helpful, Willow couldn't allow this chance to slip away. Gathering courage, she stood.

"Jason, do you have a moment?"

Both men stared at her.

"Willow—" Dr. Turner ventured.

She waved off his concern. "Everything's fine. Jason?"

He cleared his throat. Raked his good fingers through his hair. "Y–yes."

"We can sit outside so Doc can lock up. I believe it's past closing time?"

Dr. Turner hesitated, clearly contemplating whether or not to intervene.

"Yes, outside's fine." Jason nodded to Dr. Turner before making his way onto the porch.

Hardly believing this was happening, but trusting the calm that remained, Willow followed.

They settled onto the bench as an uncomfortable silence set in.

"So, Amelia and Lucas had a baby," Jason remarked.

"She's adopted. Her mother gave her up."

Though she hadn't said it, the unintended concept of abandonment became the elephant in the room.

Jason cleared his throat again. "Oh. That's nice."

"How's Darlene?"

He ran his hand around his neck. "Good."

Only good, huh. Not great. Might all not be so dandy in paradise?

"I don't begrudge anymore that you've made a life for yourself with Darlene. I've let go of the bitterness I felt when you left."

His head jolted up. "Really?"

She let her shoulders relax as she nudged her sandalled toe against a fallen geranium on the path. "God revealed to me that, by holding onto the hurt, I was only causing myself more pain. But that's not all. He showed me a way through the hurt. He provided me with healing in ways I would never have expected. He showed me there was meaning in what I'd considered my worst wound."

That she could say those words with complete sincerity left her dumbstruck. But they were true. God had done amazing things in healing her heart.

His jaw went slack as he shook his head. "I was sure you'd never forgive me—that you would hold a grudge forever."

"For a while, I did. But that only dug me deeper into a hole of self-pity." Though she'd never believed she could smile at him again, she did. "Do you know what, Jason? When I thought my life was over, God revealed a better plan for me. I was sure I'd blown my chances, but I was wrong. I'd heard people say our Lord's capable of doing far more than any of us could imagine or think. I didn't believe that until recently."

His eyes narrowed as if he still didn't believe her.

So she waved a hand. "Not only did He assure me there was a way through my nightmare but He also brought the right people to help me along the way."

"The man you were with?" He shifted, dragging his feet under the bench and gripping the seat with his good hand. "Darlene said she saw you with a man one day near the uni."

This time, Willow's mouth opened and shut like a fish. What? Darlene had seen her and Declan? Get out of here!

She finally found her tongue. "I've found a man who loves me."

Silence passed. The breeze rustled the bucket of geraniums, the fallen one skittering closer to her along the walk. She stooped to pick it up, savouring the beauty in its brokenness. Before eyeing him.

What was he thinking? Did he hold any remorse over what he'd done to her?

He moved both hands to his lap, stared at them, lifted his gaze. "I'm glad. I didn't mean to hurt you. I did love you."

"But you loved Darlene more."

His jaw tensed, released with a huff of his breath. "I'm sorry. You and I should never have married."

"I know that now."

Although her heart broke a little, it didn't matter that he'd hurt her. It didn't matter that at one time she'd planned to never see him again. He'd strayed in his walk with God, choosing the lust of his heart over faithfulness in their marriage, signalling a far deeper spiritual struggle.

He was the loser in all of this.

But God was willing to leave the entire flock to seek out the one wanderer.

In this case, that lost sheep and her betrayer were one and the same.

She leaned towards him, summoning all the grace she could muster. "I'm still not sure what happened between us. When we met, I was convinced God had brought you to be my husband for the rest of our lives. I'd never been surer of anything. Discovering I'd been wrong devastated me. But God can use what we label as a mistake for His glory. If you see our marriage as a mistake, trust me, putting the whole situation in His hands will set you free."

"The way it's set you free."

"Exactly."

He rested his good hand on his knee, his bad one still tucked safely in his lap. "I'm glad you've reached a place where you feel at peace."

It was a simple statement, yet it said a great deal. He'd created a barrier to protect himself against guilt. And he wasn't ready to face the Lord to whom he'd once entrusted his soul. Saddened, she could only pray for him.

Satisfied she'd said everything she needed to say, she stood and held her hand out. "I hope things go well for you, Jason. I really do."

He hesitated, staring at her outstretched hand as if it contained a concealed weapon. She didn't blame him. She *had* shot daggers at him, but that was before. Then his expression softened, and he took it.

"Goodbye, Willow."

"Goodbye, Jason."

As she walked to her car, although her heart was heavy for him, a lightness lifted her step. With God's strength, she'd faced him and not allowed him to hurt her again.

Praise for God overflowed from her heart.

DECLAN'S STOMACH churned as he pulled up to Willow's house. He shut off the engine, his hands rigid on the steering wheel as he gathered his thoughts. He'd had to resist the urge to go to her after Amelia told him Jason had shown up at the clinic unannounced, but since he'd been in the middle of a job, it'd been almost impossible to leave. His new partner, John, was sick, and so Declan had to get Mrs. Lowry's power reconnected before he could dash off.

His concern deepened when he learned Willow had asked to speak with Jason. What had she been thinking?

Closing his eyes, he leaned back against the headrest. He had to believe she'd known what she was doing, but her exposing herself to fresh hurt and risking old wounds being ripped open was the worst thing he could imagine.

Trust Me.

He blinked. In panic, he'd forgotten her greatest shield went with her—the Holy Spirit. Hadn't he prayed that a shield would be placed around her if ever this situation happened? *I'm sorry, Lord.*

He pushed his door open and climbed out. When she greeted him with a smile, his every muscle loosened. Wasting no time, he took her in his arms. "How are you, sweetheart?"

"I'm good." Pulling back from him, she tipped her head and looked into his eyes. "Were you worried?"

He exhaled. Averted his gaze. Ran his hand over his hair. "I was."

She placed her hand on his cheek, turning his gaze back to her. "There was no need. Come sit down. Would you like a drink?"

He accepted, though he had little interest in anything but hearing what the love of his life had to say. He followed her to the kitchen.

"Here we are." She handed him a tall glass of iced tea. "Let's sit on the back porch."

Once outside, they sat together on a double couch, her potted plants flourishing on the railing, salt-scented air embracing them. Facing her, he took her hand. "Tell me what happened."

She curled her fingers into his. They weren't trembling. "I

was surprised to see him. He was surprised to see me, too. He thought he could get in and out without bumping into me."

"He was wrong."

"But you know what?" She nestled in closer, hugging his arm to her side. "I believe it was a God thing because now I feel free of him. I said what I needed to say. I told him I don't feel a grudge against him and that God had a better plan."

Declan chuckled. "I bet that went down well."

Her eyes twinkled. "Yeah, kind of." Her expression sobered. "I don't think he and Darlene are happy."

"I guess that's not a surprise. He acted out of God's will."

She dipped her head to rest against his shoulder, a soft sigh slipping loose. "I feel sorry for him. I'm going to pray he returns to faith and finds peace."

He breathed in, savouring the scent of her citrusy perfume and soaking in the blessed peace about her. "That's admirable of you, my darling. I'm so glad you're okay."

Raising her head enough to look at him, she rolled her eyes. "You and me both, believe me! But God was good, and He protected my heart."

"Just like we prayed."

She hugged an arm around his waist, sighing. "Yes."

His face stretched in a grin. He stroked her hair. "I'm sure he regretted leaving you when he saw you. But his loss is my gain."

She leaned up and kissed his lips and then snuggled against his shoulder. A companionable silence followed before she spoke. "The most important thing was telling him I'm not angry anymore, I forgive him."

"That's no small thing." He rubbed her arm. "I'm glad you got the chance to tell him."

"So am I."

CHAPTER
TWENTY

On a beautiful, starlit spring evening, after spending the day exploring Sydney, Declan took Willow on a sunset dinner cruise on Sydney Harbour to celebrate her birthday. During the six months since they'd started dating, he'd fallen deeper and deeper in love with her, and tonight, he'd propose.

He wanted the evening to be perfect. Storms had been predicted, but when they arrived at Circular Quay at five o'clock, only a few clouds hovered on the horizon.

Despite being out and about all day, she looked gorgeous in white casual pants, a coral cami with a loose sparkly silver overshirt, and heels. She made any outfit look spectacular, but he particularly liked this one.

He showed their tickets, and they were welcomed on board. Canapes were being served on the superyacht's upper deck, and he placed a steadying hand on the small of her back as they climbed the stairs. A three-piece band was already playing soft dinner music, while male waiters in crisp white shirts and black bow ties offered the guests gourmet appetisers on silver trays.

Similarly dressed waitresses offered an assortment of drinks. They both chose sparkling apple juice in fluted glasses. With drinks in hand, they headed for a railing and stood, eating and drinking until the captain welcomed everyone on board and the boat cast away from the dock.

They sailed under the Harbour Bridge, past the Opera House, and were then served their main course. He chose the eye fillet with sautéed vegetables and mushroom sauce. She chose the salmon and salad. As if to complement the delicious meals, the sun set in a spectacular fashion, and the lights of Sydney came on and dazzled while they dined.

Afterwards, he invited her to dance. Unlike the high-energy dancing at the bush dance, this time they danced a slow rhythm foxtrot. It was the most romantic thing he'd ever done. Holding her close, swaying to the music while the boat rose and fell in the slight swell was the stuff memories were made of. But how did one propose while surrounded by others? How could he drop to one knee, convey his love, and ask her to marry him?

Then the band took a short break, and everyone else on board headed for the inside bar, leaving them alone on deck. Without hesitation, he dropped to one knee, took her hands, and gazed up into her eyes.

"Willow, you're the most amazing person, and I've fallen madly and deeply in love with you. I can't think of anyone else I want to spend the rest of my life with. Willow Kelly, will you do me the honour of becoming my wife?"

Her eyes widened, and he held his breath as his heart pounded.

Was it too soon? Was she ready to take this step? He'd prayed about it and felt at peace, but perhaps he'd gotten it wrong.

But then, a smile broke loose, and she shouted a resounding, "Yes! I love you Declan, and I want to marry you."

Yes!

She pulled him to his feet and threw her arms around him. His arms encircled her waist, and he swirled her around.

Setting her down, he pulled the small ring box from his pocket. He'd done it all wrong. It should have been out, ready to slide onto her finger, but did it matter? Opening the black velvet case, he removed the white gold solitaire diamond ring and slipped it onto her long, slim finger and beamed. It looked gorgeous.

"Declan! It's beautiful. Thank you." She launched herself against him again, almost knocking him overboard. Her lips found his in a kiss passionate and warm. How he loved this woman.

They spent the rest of the cruise in each other's arms, swaying to the music, gazing at the lights of Sydney. A magical evening. If only they were already married. She said she didn't want a big wedding. Something small and intimate. Just immediate family and close friends. And she didn't want a long engagement. Having spent the last six months getting to know each other, they were ready to commit.

Tonight, they were staying with his mother since it was too far to drive back to Water's Edge. His mother's steps towards healing and wholeness had been slow, but she was progressing. She'd even booked a holiday to Tasmania with her friend, Vera. And she was considering selling the house.

He needed to discuss that with Willow. He wanted to start their married life in their own home, where memories of her previous, short-lived marriage wouldn't lurk in every nook and cranny. She loved her little house, so he prayed she'd see merit in starting afresh. But he wouldn't broach the topic tonight. Tonight was for celebrating their engagement.

The boat docked, and they were almost the last to disembark. In no hurry to go home, he suggested a stroll along the quay. She agreed, and with his arm wrapped around her, they strolled towards the Opera House.

They bought ice creams and sat on the steps while buskers played and boats sailed by. He nuzzled her neck and whispered words of love.

Finally, it was time to leave. They hailed a taxi to drive them to the car park. She snuggled close in the back seat. Climbing into his ute ten minutes later seemed an anticlimax. At least he'd cleaned it, and no wrappers or Coke cans littered the cab. And he'd shampooed the mats and hung a freshener from the rear-view mirror.

Seated, he faced her. Reached for her hand. "I love you, Willow. Thank you for agreeing to marry me."

Her eyes shone as she clasped his hand tighter. "Thank you for loving me. Because of you, I can smile again."

EPILOGUE

Three months later

As Mum and Amelia helped her into her wedding gown and did up the twenty tiny pearl buttons on the back, Willow gazed at her reflection in the full-length mirror.

She'd designed and made the gown, a simple sweetheart bodice in satin and French tulle. She loved the soft and dreamy feel of it, and the skirt fell beautifully. When she'd said she simply intended to wear a nice dress, Mum claimed that was nonsense. "You may have been married before, but Declan hasn't. Don't you think you should dazzle him?"

Thinking of it like that, Willow agreed. And it had been the right decision.

"Doesn't she look gorgeous, Amelia?" Mum's eyes glistened as she adjusted the skirt.

Amelia nodded. "She sure does."

As the matron of honour, Amelia was wearing a sky-blue, satin mid-length dress. Since Lucas was Declan's best man, Charlotte had been tasked with minding baby Ivy and didn't mind in the least.

"How are you doing?" Mum rubbed Willow's arm.

"I'm doing great."

When Willow clamped a hand over Mum's, Mum stepped forward and hugged her. "I'm so happy for you. Declan's a wonderful man, and you two are going to have a wonderful marriage."

"If it's anything like yours and Dad's, I'll be more than happy."

"That's such a nice thing to say. Dad and I *have* been blessed, and I pray that blessing over you, too."

"Thank you, Mum." Willow dabbed under her eye with a corner of a tissue. "We should be going, or Declan might think I've changed my mind. Is Dad ready?"

"Yes, he is." His deep voice came from the doorway.

Willow looked past Mum, her heart overflowing. "Wonderful. Let's go."

THE SONG he and Willow had chosen began playing. Declan's chest constricted, and his breathing slowed. It was time. He looked to Lucas, grinned, and then turned his gaze to the dunes where his bride would emerge. His heart pumped. His hands grew clammy.

Amelia came into view, and Lucas beamed. Not surprising, as she looked gorgeous in her sky-blue dress. But Willow. Willow. Never had Declan seen such beauty. And her gown— perfection. Soft, flowing, and feminine. He swallowed the lump in his throat as she drew closer. He couldn't take his eyes off her. And then she was beside him. Her dad gave a nod and placed her hand into Declan's. He squeezed it and smiled into her beautiful face. Then, tucking her hand into the crook of his arm, he turned her to face Pastor Noah.

It was like a dream. Pastor Noah welcomed everyone to the wedding of Declan John Ross and Willow Maree Kelley. He thanked God for the beautiful setting and for bringing the two of them together. They sang their favourite hymn, 'How Great Thou Art,' and then he addressed them. What he was saying was important, so Declan forced himself to focus, although he just wanted to say, 'I do'.

"Declan and Willow, it's my privilege today to preside over your wedding. You stand here today not only to declare your love for each other but also for God, the designer of this great institution of marriage. Seeing you both grow in your faith and your love for each other has been a blessing, and I'm over-joyed God has brought you to this moment. Let's pray."

Declan caught her gaze before bowing his head, the tenderness in her smile sending warmth trickling through his whole body.

"Lord, we thank You that You've brought us here to this moment on this day. We love Declan and Willow, and we're excited for them as they enter holy matrimony. We pray this commitment being made today will honour and glorify You for their lifetime. May the love of Christ be evident in their union, and may they together be true witnesses to Your love to those around them. Lord, we pray these things in Jesus' precious name. Amen."

Raising his head, Pastor Noah gave them a warm smile before announcing that Amelia would now bring the Bible reading.

She stepped to the microphone before the white timber trellis covered with pink rosebuds and cleared her voice. "Today's reading comes from 1 Corinthians 13, verses 1 to 13." She looked down at her Bible. "'If I speak in the tongues of men or of angels, but do not have love, I am only a resounding gong or a clanging cymbal. If I have the gift of prophecy and can fathom all mysteries and all knowledge, and if I have a faith that can move mountains, but do not have love, I am nothing. If I give all I possess to the poor and give over my body to hardship that I may boast, but do not have love, I gain nothing.

"'Love is patient, love is kind. It does not envy, it does not boast, it is not proud. It does not dishonour others, it is not self-seeking, it is not easily angered, it keeps no record of wrongs. Love does not delight in evil but rejoices with the truth. It always protects, always trusts, always hopes, always perseveres. Love never fails.'"

Declan's heart quickened as the words reached deep into his soul and he determined to love Willow with everything he had.

Amelia continued. "'And now these three remain: faith, hope and love. But the greatest of these is love.'"

Closing her Bible, she smiled at him and Willow. "God bless you both."

They'd written their own vows, and as Declan took Willow's hand, he looked deep into her beautiful eyes. This was the moment he'd been waiting for all his life. "James 1, verse 17 says that every good and perfect gift comes from above. Willow, you're truly a gift from God, and I promise to spend the rest of my life treating you as such. I'll always cherish you and never take you for granted. I'll guide and lead you as Christ leads me. I'll obey His commands and follow His teachings. I'll lead by example, with patience, kindness, and understanding. I'll be slow to anger and quick to listen. I'll be a strong spiritual leader in our home, through good times and bad, in joy and in sorrow." Pausing, he sucked in a steadying breath. "Willow, I promise to love you and to be faithful to you alone from this day forward until God calls us home. This is my solemn pledge to you and to God." He took the ring from Lucas and held her gaze. "Willow, please accept this ring as a symbol of our covenant and my undying love for you."

Her eyes misted over as he slipped the white gold wedding band onto her finger. And then it was her turn. As she took his hand and promised to love and honour him as her husband for as long as they both should live, he could hardly contain the joy bubbling inside him. And when Pastor Noah announced they were man and wife and he could kiss her, giddy happiness swept him up. Willow was now his wife, and he was 'the happiest man alive'.

Taking her in his arms, he lowered his mouth and kissed her with all the love in his heart. Everyone laughed and cheered, and when he pulled back from their kiss, the love sparkling from her eyes enveloped him.

SOFT PIANO MUSIC played in the background while they signed the register under the rose-petalled trellis. It all seemed like a dream to Willow as they smiled for the cameras and kissed and laughed again and again. But when Pastor Noah stood and introduced them as Mr. and Mrs. Declan and Willow Ross, it wasn't a dream. It was real.

They held the reception under a white marquee on the beach where a range of local native flowers adorned rows of tastefully decorated tables. The luncheon, provided by Charlotte and her staff, featured a selection of gourmet finger food followed by a choice of grilled chicken seasoned with garlic, lemon, and butter and served with steamed broccolini, or a baby rack of lamb coated with a blend of herbs and spices and served with sautéed baby carrots and potato croquettes.

All through the afternoon, Willow could barely keep her gaze off her husband, so handsome in his cream suit, and the smile on his face warmed her heart. But she *did* notice Doc and Charlotte were spending a lot of time together, cooing over baby Ivy.

When it came time to leave, Willow slipped her arm around Declan's waist while he thanked everyone for coming. As her gaze moved around their family and friends, overwhelming gratitude to God welled within her for their love and support. How things had changed in the last twelve months. Never would she have believed she could be so happy.

They said their goodbyes, kicked off their shoes, and walked arm in arm across the sand to a waiting limo.

In the back seat, Willow laughed with Declan at the sound of tin cans bouncing along the road behind them.

Turning her face to his, he grinned and kissed her with unbridled passion.

LET *them give thanks to the Lord for His unfailing love and His wonderful deeds for mankind, for He satisfies the thirsty and fills the hungry with good things (Psalm 107:8–9).*

NOTE FROM THE AUTHOR

I hope you enjoyed "Because of You" and were blessed by it. Book 3 in The Water's Edge Series, "With You Beside Me", is coming soon! Keep an eye out for it, but in the meantime, please enjoy the draft Prologue which you'll find below.

To ensure you don't miss any of my new releases, why not join my Readers' list (http://www.julietteduncan.-com/linkspage/282748) ? You'll also receive a free thank-you copy of "Hank and Sarah - A Love Story", a clean love story with God at the center.

Enjoyed "Because of You"? You can make a big difference. Help other people find this book by writing a review and telling them why you liked it. Honest reviews of my books help bring them to the attention of other readers just like yourself, and I'd be very grateful if you could spare just five minutes to leave a review (it can be as short as you like) on the book's Amazon page.

Keep reading for your bonus chapter of "With You Beside Me".

Blessings,
Juliette

With You Beside Me
Prologue

AMELIA KELLEY BECAME INSTANTLY alert at the sound of her daughter's cry. Ever since adopting Ivy two years earlier, she'd been a light sleeper, however, the toddler's cry was different tonight.

A shiver of dread ran up her spine.

She made her way quickly to Ivy's room, gathering her distraught daughter into her arms.

"Ssshhhh, it's all right, Mummy's here." Settling into the rocking chair, her heart pounded. Ivy was burning up. Usually, a hug from Amelia and Ivy would calm her quickly, but tonight, Ivy's cry was intensifying.

"Amelia?"

She raised her head. Lucas stood in the doorway, bleary eyed, but clearly concerned.

"She has a fever." Amelia's heart crumbled as she looked at her daughter. She'd never felt so helpless.

Lucas placed his hand on Ivy's small forehead.

Even in the darkness, she saw his face pale.

Ivy's cries grew increasingly desperate.

"We need to get to Dr. Turner," Amelia said, her voice breaking.

"I'll call him now." Lucas was already headed to the bedroom for his phone.

Amelia's hands shook as she carried Ivy downstairs, speaking softly to her to try to soothe her, but to no avail.

By the time they were out the door, Amelia's heart beat in her throat. As a trained nurse, she was used to handling emergencies. But this, this was different. This was their precious daughter.

"Please, God, help our little girl," she whispered as Lucas backed the car out of the driveway. "Protect Ivy and keep us calm. This is all in Your hands, but, Lord, I'm so scared…"

Lucas's knuckles turned white as he gripped the steering wheel, his lips also moving in silent prayer.

Dr. Turner met them the moment they pulled up outside the clinic. Good thing he lived next door.

Drawing a deep breath, Amelia blinked rapidly as she unbuckled her distraught daughter from her car seat.

Dr. Turner ushered them into the exam room. "I believe you haven't been able to calm her down."

"She's never been so disconsolate." Amelia's lips twisted. She flattened them to keep the wobble out. "She's burning up."

She jigged and soothed her daughter, and finally Ivy calmed enough to allow the doctor to examine her.

Ivy stared at them, her eyes red, hiccuping as she sucked her thumb and hugged her teddy.

"You both look shaken. Why don't you sit in the waiting room for a few minutes and catch your breath?" Dr. Turner gave a reassuring smile.

Amelia's motherly instincts protested at the thought of leaving Ivy, but she reluctantly handed her over and allowed Lucas to lead her out of the exam room.

She sunk into one of the chairs, unable to stop shaking. Lucas wrapped his arm around her shoulders. She leaned into his chest, the smell of his familiar scent comforting her.

"She's going to be all right," he whispered.

"Yes, I know." She brushed tears from her cheeks. "But I can't help being worried."

He rubbed her shoulder. "I know."

"We should call the family. Let them know what's happening."

"You're right. I'll make the calls." Lucas pulled his phone out and called first his parents, and then his sister and brother-in-law. They all promised to pray.

When Dr. Turner emerged from the exam room holding Ivy, Amelia jumped to her feet.

"What is it, Dr. Turner? What's wrong with her?"

He gave Ivy an affectionate pat on the cheek, earning him an exhausted smile before he transferred her to Amelia. Ivy melted into her arms.

"I gave her some medication that should keep her comfortable through the night. I'll write you a prescription for more should you need it."

Amelia glanced at Lucas before looking back at Dr. Turner. "What do you think it is? It's not an ordinary fever, is it?"

The doctor's mouth flattened into a grim line. "I believe it's more serious than that. We'll get some tests done and then we'll know more. The waiting will be hard, but until we get the tests done and the results back, I'm reluctant to surmise."

Amelia read between the lines. She forced a wobbly smile. "We understand."

She was in a daze as she listened to the doctor's homecare instructions, her mind moving into prayer once more.

"I don't know what's going on, but You do, Lord. We entrust Ivy into Your care. Watch over our little daughter, and give us peace."

Find Water's Edge Series here.

OTHER BOOKS BY JULIETTE DUNCAN

Find all of Juliette Duncan's books on her website:

www.julietteduncan.com/library

Water's Edge Series

When I Met You

A barmaid searching for purpose, a youth pastor searching for love

Because of You

When dreams are shattered, can hope be re-found?

A Sunburned Land Series

A mature-age romance series

Slow Road to Love

A divorced reporter on a remote assignment. An alluring cattleman who captures her heart...

Slow Path to Peace

With their lives stripped bare, can Serena and David find peace?

Slow Ride Home

He's a cowboy who lives his life with abandon. She's spirited and fiercely independent...

Slow Dance at Dusk

A death, a wedding, and a change of plans...

Slow Trek to Triumph

A road trip, a new romance, and a new start...

The Shadows Series

A jilted teacher, a charming Irishman, & the chance to escape their pasts & start again.

Lingering Shadows

Facing the Shadows

Beyond the Shadows

Secrets and Sacrifice

A Highland Christmas

True Love Series

Tender Love

Tested Love

Tormented Love

Triumphant Love

Precious Love Series

Forever Cherished

Forever Faithful

Forever His

A Time For Everything Series

A mature-age Christian Romance series

A Time to Treasure

She lost her husband and misses him dearly. He lost his wife but is ready to move on. Will a chance meeting in a foreign city change their lives forever?

A Time to Care

They've tied the knot, but will their love last the distance?

A Time to Abide

When grief hovers like a cloud, will the sun ever shine again for Wendy?

A Time to Rejoice

He's never forgiven himself for the accident that killed his mother. Can he find forgiveness and true love?

Transformed by Love Christian Romance Series

Because We Loved

Because We Forgave

Because We Dreamed

Because We Believed

Because We Cared

Billionaires with Heart Series

Her Kind-Hearted Billionaire

A reluctant billionaire, a grieving young woman, and the trip *that changes their lives forever...*

Her Generous Billionaire

A grieving billionaire, a devoted solo mother, and a woman determined to sabotage their relationship...

Her Disgraced Billionaire

A billionaire in jail, a nurse who cares, and the challenge that changes their lives forever...

Her Compassionate Billionaire

A widowed billionaire with three young children. A replacement nanny who helps change his life...

The Potter's House Books...

Stories of hope, redemption, and second chances. *The Homecoming*

Can she surrender a life of fame and fortune to find true love?

Blessings of Love

She's going on mission to help others. He's going to win her heart.

The Hope We Share

Can the Master Potter work in Rachel and Andrew's hearts and give them a second chance at love?

The Love Abounds

Can the Master Potter work in Megan's heart and save her marriage?

Love's Healing Touch

A doctor in need of healing. A nurse in need of love.

Melody of Love

She's fleeing an abusive relationship, he's grieving his wife's death...

Whispers of Hope

He's struggling to accept his new normal. She's losing her

patience...

Promise of Peace

She's disillusioned and troubled. He has a secret...

Heroes Of Eastbrooke Christian Suspense Series

Safe in His Arms

SOME SAY HE'S HIDING. HE SAYS HE'S SURVIVING

Under His Watch

HE'LL STOP AT NOTHING TO PROTECT THOSE HE LOVES. NOTHING.

Within His Sight

SHE'LL STOP AT NOTHING TO GET A STORY. HE'LL SCALE THE HIGHEST MOUNTAIN TO RESCUE HER.

Freed by His Love

HE'S DRIVEN AND DETERMINED. SHE'S BROKEN AND SCARED.

Stand Alone Christian Romantic Suspense

Leave Before He Kills You

When his face grew angry, I knew he could murder...

The Madeleine Richards Series

Although the 3 book series is intended mainly for pre-teen/Middle Grade girls, it's been read and enjoyed by people of all ages. Here's what one reader had to say about it: *"Juliette has a fabulous way of bringing her characters to life. Maddy is at typical teenager with authentic views and actions that truly make it feel like you are feeling her pain and angst. You want to enter into her situation and make everything better. Mom and soon to be dad respond to her with love and gentle persuasion while maintaining their faith and trust in Jesus, whom they know, will give them wisdom as they continue on their lives journey. Appropriate for teenage readers but any age can enjoy." Reader*

ABOUT THE AUTHOR

Juliette Duncan is a *USA Today* bestselling author of Christian romance stories that 'touch the heart and soul'. She lives in Brisbane, Australia and writes Christian fiction that encourages a deeper faith in a world that seems to have lost its way. Most of her stories include an element of romance, because who doesn't love a good love story? But the main love story in each of her books is always God's amazing, unconditional love for His wayward children.

Juliette and her husband enjoy spending time with their five adult children, eight grandchildren, and their elderly, long-haired dachshund, Chipolata (Chip for short). When not writing, Juliette and her husband love exploring the wonderful world they live in.

Connect with Juliette:

Email: author@julietteduncan.com

Website: www.julietteduncan.com

Facebook: www.facebook.com/JulietteDuncanAuthor

Made in the USA
Coppell, TX
24 September 2024

37650802R00116